SHOWDOWN AT SHADOW JUNCTION

JOANNA WAYNE

D0053146

 **HARLEQUIN**® INTRIGUE®

To my family, who keep me grounded; my friends, who keep me entertained and sane; and to my fantastic editor, Denise Zaza, who lets me keep creating Texas ranching families like the Daltons. Love and thanks to all.

ISBN-13: 978-0-373-69830-1

Showdown at Shadow Junction

Copyright © 2015 by Jo Ann Vest

Recycling programs for this product may not exist in your area.

Printed in U.S.A.

www.Harlequin.com

"I think it's time for the second kiss."

His good judgment vanished as Jade's arms wrapped around his neck. He captured her lips with his and he was done for. The thrill sent blood rushing to his head, making him dizzy with desire.

He leaned against the door frame and pulled her against him as the kiss deepened. Her lips opened and the taste of her rocked his soul. When his lungs ached from lack of air, he held her even tighter, nibbling her lips and then trailing her neck with kisses. Fighting not to explode, he finally came to his senses.

She was tipsy, vulnerable, her life mired in uncertainty. A kiss was one thing. But making love would take things to a new level, good or bad, that would leave no room for going back.

He couldn't risk it, not with her life in his hands.

Joanna Wayne began her professional writing career in 1994. Now, more than fifty published books later, Joanna has gained a worldwide following with her cutting-edge romantic suspense and Texas family series such as Sons of Troy Ledger and the Big "D" Dads series. Joanna currently resides in a small community north of Houston, Texas, with her husband. You may write Joanna at PO Box 852, Montgomery, Texas 77356, or connect with her at joannawayne.com.

Books by Joanna Wayne

HARLEQUIN INTRIGUE

Big "D" Dads: The Daltons

Trumped Up Charges

Unrepentant Cowboy

Hard Ride to Dry Gulch

Midnight Rider

Showdown at Shadow Junction

Sons of Troy Ledger

Cowboy Swagger

Genuine Cowboy

AK-Cowboy

Cowboy Fever

Cowboy Conspiracy

Big "D" Dads

Son of a Gun

Live Ammo

Big Shot

Visit the Author Profile page at Harlequin.com for more titles.

CAST OF CHARACTERS

Jade Dalton—Only daughter and youngest child of R. J. Dalton. A corporate event planner in New York City who finds herself in imminent danger when her client is murdered.

Booker Knox—Navy SEAL back in the United States on leave. He'll do whatever it takes to keep Jade alive.

Quaid Vaquero—A world-renowned jewelry designer until he turns up dead.

R. J. Dalton—Jade's biological father owns the Dry Gulch Ranch just outside Dallas. He is certain the safest place for Jade is on his ranch.

Winston Fielding—A bulldog of a homicide detective with the NYPD. He won't give up until he discovers the truth.

Javier Aranda—A longtime friend of Vaquero.

Reggie Lassiter—Off duty police officer hired by Jade to protect Quaid Vaquero and his jewelry.

Mark Lassiter—Reggie's brother and the owner of the security agency.

Zoe Aranda—Vaquero's assistant and longtime friend.

Chapter One

"This is the crown of my collection, the surprise revelation I promised for my final US showing."

Jade Dalton stared in awe at the necklace. A cascade of flawless diamonds, separated by pure green emeralds dangled from Quaid Vaquero's fingertips.

"It's magnificent. It's…" She paused. "Mere words cannot do it justice."

"I'm glad you're impressed. It took over a year to find the perfect gems, almost three hundred of them, hand cut and set in platinum."

"I'm afraid to even ask the price," Jade said.

Quaid smiled. "Two twenty-five. No price bickering. I won't part with it for anyone who doesn't appreciate not only its quality but its beauty and artistic value."

"Two hundred twenty-five thousand?"

He smiled as if amused by her naiveté. "Two hundred twenty-five million, my sweet."

"You're kidding, right?"

"Not at all."

"Now you're scaring me. What on earth are you doing with this in your hotel suite? I need to call someone from security immediately. I think Officer Reggie Lassiter is in charge tonight. He'll make sure this is placed in the showroom where he and his security detail can guard it."

"Relax. No one knows it's here but the two of us. Besides, it's well insured."

"Still, this isn't wise, Mr. Vaquero. Had you mentioned this to me, I would never have approved it. Neither would Reggie. And if I were your insurance provider, I would be in a state of pure panic."

"A piece such as this is created to be worn by an equally beautiful woman, not locked away. And not to change the subject, but you've worked closely with me for two weeks now. Don't you think it's time you start calling me Quaid?"

"Quaid it is. But I work *for* you, not *with* you. And as your event planner, I am very nervous now."

"I can tell." He put a hand to the small of her back and nudged her toward a full-length tilt mirror. The mirror support and frame were dark polished wood and, like everything else in his luxury suite, looked antique and no doubt far more expensive than it actually was.

"Look at yourself," Quaid urged. "I've never seen you this flustered."

Her nerves were edgy and with good reason. People didn't just walk around a New York hotel with a two-hundred-million-dollar-plus necklace in their pocket. Her ex-stepfather number three had worked as a hotel food manager. He'd told her plenty of stories about professional hotel thieves robbing guests, though admittedly, this was usually when they were out of their room. But you never knew when thieves would become emboldened.

Who'd inspire risk taking more than a world-renowned jewelry designer?

She turned and looked into the mirror, but it wasn't her uneasiness that she saw reflected in the glass. It was the incredibly handsome Spaniard standing behind her with his dark, soul-searing eyes and seductive glances. The man who had mesmerized her for the past two weeks.

His hands brushed her shoulders as he fastened the sparkling work of art around her neck. The shimmering jewels fell into the swell of her cleavage just above the spaghetti-strap red cocktail dress she'd splurged a month's wages on for tonight's event.

"It's breathtakingly beautiful," she murmured truthfully.

"It's *you* who is breathtaking, Jade. The jewels merely accentuate your natural beauty."

Charm oozed from Quaid every time he opened his mouth. Yet she sensed something more poignant in his manner tonight. Probably just more relaxed because it was the end of his visit to America.

Or could he possibly be interested in a romantic interlude now that their business association was reaching its conclusion? Would he invite her to visit him in his lavish lakeside villa in Spain or perhaps to sail around the Greek Islands on his massive yacht?

Don't even go there, she cautioned herself. The man had supermodels and royalty at his beck and call.

Tonight's event promised to be his best-attended showing to date. His reputation had skyrocketed since his arrival in New York. Wearing jewelry from Quaid Vaquero's collection had become the rage among the ultra-wealthy society set.

Quaid put his mouth to her ear as if they were exchanging secrets. "I would be honored if you'd wear the necklace this evening."

His warm breath on her neck was intoxicating. His offer was incredibly tempting. It was also a terrible idea. Her job was to make certain the night went without a snag, not to model and play princess.

"I'd love to wear this necklace, Quaid. As it is, you might have to pry it from my neck. But anything this valuable must be under one of the museum-quality glass domes for tonight's showing."

"You've assured me there will be cameras and plain-clothes security personnel in abundance."

"Yes, but there are other drawbacks to my wearing it."

"Such as?"

Quaid's fingers trailed seductively from the back of her neck to her bare shoulders. He was not making this easy.

"The necklace must be displayed appropriately so that your potential customers can examine it thoroughly through the glass and hopefully request to try it on."

"Point made. But let me enjoy it on you for the moment."

"For a moment," she acquiesced, "but we really should be going soon. I'm sure the first of your guests are already arriving. They're here to meet you as much as they are to see your creations."

"They can wait. First, I have a gift for you."

"Honestly, that's not necessary."

"Gifts are never necessary, Jade. They should always come from the heart."

He turned, tugged her around to face him and took both her hands in his. Her heart pounded. He was going to kiss her. This was a working assignment. She should step away.

Instead, she lifted her lips toward his. The moment was interrupted by a light tapping.

"Room service."

Quaid didn't hide his annoyance as he walked over and opened the door. "I didn't order anything."

"I've got the ticket right here. Room 2333. Champagne for two."

"Someone wishing you luck," Jade said, "not that you'll need it. Your talent speaks for itself."

Quaid stepped aside as the young, uniformed hotel employee pushed in a table holding a bottle of chilled champagne.

The attendant lifted the bottle from the crystal bucket for them to examine. Jade recognized the label and knew from previous events at this hotel that the champagne sold for over five hundred dollars a bottle.

"Can you at least tell me who sent this," Quaid asked the server, "so that I'll know whom to thank?"

The young man looked at the ticket again. "The only information on here is that it's for Mr. Quaid Vaquero at this room number. No charge to you. If you call room service, they may be able to tell you."

"Yes, I'll check with them later."

"Shall I pop the cork and pour?" the server asked.

"You're already here," Quaid said, "so you may as well."

Quaid turned back to Jade, took her hand with an unexpected familiarity and led her to the window that offered a magnificent view of the city. "I could have done without the interruption."

"Yes, but you have a very generous friend," Jade said. Odd timing, though, unless the person who had it delivered knew he was unveiling the necklace to her in his suite.

The cork popped loudly.

Quaid ignored it and slipped his arm around her waist. "I expected to hate New York, but I have loved every minute of my visit. I owe most of that to you."

"You give me far too much credit. New York has a

magic all its own. I was only sixteen when I first visited
here with my mother. I knew then I was a big-city girl."

"Can I get you anything else?" the server asked.

"That will be all." Quaid turned back to him, pulled
a money clip from his right front pocket and placed a tip
on the cart. He waited until they were alone again before
he handed Jade a flute of the sparkling bubbly.

"To successful ventures of business and of the heart,"
he said, lifting his glass.

Jade clinked hers with his, though she was afraid to
even guess what he meant by the last part of the toast.

Now that she thought about it, she wondered if he had
ordered the champagne himself. This supposedly im-
promptu meeting was feeling more like an orchestrated
seduction scene by the minute.

What was he looking for from her? A sexual hookup
on his last night in the States? One-night stands were
not her style.

But what if he offered more? A visit to his lavish Barcelona villa to get know her better? A few weeks on his
yacht?

They'd almost finished their champagne before Quaid
reached into the pocket of his tailor-made sport coat. He
pulled out a small shiny red box tied with silver ribbon,
the trademark wrapping for a custom-made Vaquero jeweled creation.

Surely he wasn't planning to give her anything that
pricey—unless he really was interested in pursuing a relationship. As tempting as it all sounded, she didn't know
that she was interested. She loved her life just as it was.

Quaid handed her the box.

She finished off her champagne, suddenly too nervous
to even tug the ribbon loose from the package. Finally,

she eased the silver bow from around the corners and lifted the lid. She stared, too overwhelmed to speak.

"Do you like them?"

"I love them. How could I not?" She gingerly lifted one of the earrings from its nest of black velvet. A dangling emerald shimmered with a thousand pinpoints of light.

"I don't know what to say. They're exquisite. I've never owned anything like this, but…"

"Say thank you," Quaid suggested. "I designed and had them made especially for you."

She was stunned. Emotionally touched. Light-headed.

"They're absolutely exquisite, but I really can't accept…" The emerald began to dance in front of her eyes. Her tongue grew thick, slurring her words.

She reached for the back of a chair to steady herself as the room began to spin. A second later her legs gave way and she crumpled to the floor.

"Jade, what's wrong?"

She tried to answer but couldn't form the words. Quaid lifted her in his arms and carried her to the bed. As he laid her down, she felt his hands at her throat.

She closed her eyes and when she opened them, he was floating above her in an opaque mist as if he were being swallowed by the suffocating vapor.

He wasn't alone. Reggie Lassiter was there, as well. Shadowy figures lurked in the background.

Loud voices. Reggie pointing a gun.

And then it all whirled away in a cloud as dark as midnight.

Chapter Two

R.J. Dalton stepped through the front door, sipped his coffee and stared out over his front lawn. It was getting harder and harder to recognize the place where he'd spent all his life. Almost eight decades.

His daughters-in-law, Hadley and Faith, had spent hours sprucing up the place. New flower beds bordered the freshly painted porch. A dozen or more blooming plants he couldn't name were tucked in with the morning glories, zinnias, marigolds and petunias. Hanging pots overflowed with geraniums.

Colorful pillows and cushions not only brightened the porch swing and outdoor rockers but made them a lot more comfortable.

He appreciated the effort, but still more often than not, it was flashes of the past that gripped him when he settled in his favorite rocker. The memories ran rough-shod through his mind, good and bad, hit and miss, the events in no coherent order.

His short-term memory was even less dependable. Countless times a day he walked from one room to another only to forget why or what he was looking for. Some of that he figured was just old age.

But the gaps in time, the shaky hands and the dizzy spells he chalked up to the inoperable tumor in his brain. The dang thing was growing again, according to his neurosurgeon.

Not that R.J. had any right to complain. The cancer should have killed him over a year ago. Hell, his life-style should have killed him long before he got to be an old man.

Boozing. Wild women. Aces up his sleeve. Bar fights. Not that he was proud of his past. It just was what it was and regret couldn't change it. Wallowing in guilt wouldn't change it, either, so he didn't waste his time trying.

He planned to spend his remaining days enjoying the good life he was lucky enough to have now. Four sons—Adam, Leif, Travis and Cannon—all making their homes with their families right here on the Dry Gulch Ranch, though only Cannon and his wife and baby girl, Kimmie, lived in the big house with R.J.

Sons who had no reason to give a damn about R.J., yet they'd forgiven him his sorry parenting. Or at least they were making a stab at it and doing a bang-up job of not following in his footsteps.

R.J. walked over and dropped into the old wooden rocker. The floorboards creaked as he rocked, about the only sound around this morning. Not that he minded the quiet, especially since he knew it wouldn't last for long.

One or the other of his sons, daughters-in-law or grandchildren were constantly stopping by to check on him. When they couldn't, they made sure his housekeeper and friend, Mattie Mae, was around to see that he was taken care of.

Only, Mattie Mae was off at her granddaughter's college graduation this week. Lucky her. It would take a miracle for R.J. to live long enough to see one of his grandchildren graduate from college.

The sound of a car's engine interrupted R.J.'s reverie.

He leaned forward, shielding his eyes from the sun's glare with his wrinkled right hand as he tried to figure out who was coming down the ranch road.

A surge of warmth washed through him when he recognized the silver Mercedes. Feeling much sprier than he had minutes ago, he stood and walked to the edge of the porch to greet his favorite neighbor.

Carolina Lambert stepped out of the car and started up the walk to meet him. In her early fifties, she was still one of the best-looking women in the county. Rich, smart and a damn good cook, too.

"You're mighty dressed up to be making neighborly house calls," he said.

"I'm on my way to Dallas."

"Got a date?"

"You know better than that. I have a meeting with some of the major donors for my for my Saddle-Up charity."

"How's that going?"

"It's gaining speed. I'm hoping to enlist at least a dozen additional ranchers to join the program this year. It's truly amazing what a month in the summer spent on a working ranch can do for troubled inner-city kids."

R.J. smiled. "Always the do-gooder."

"I'm blessed. It would be a travesty if I didn't share."

"So, what brings you to the Dry Gulch this morning? Not that I'm complaining, mind you."

The smile disappeared from her lips. "Let's sit," she said, joining him on the porch.

He spied a brown envelope she was holding in her right hand. "If that's bad news you're bringing, I'm not sure I want it." But he sat back down in his rocker as Carolina settled in the porch swing.

"Have you ever heard of a man named Quaid Vaquero?" she asked.

"No. Should I have?"

"He's a well-known jewelry designer from Spain."

"Last piece of jewelry I purchased was this here Timex." He pushed up the sleeve of his cotton shirt to show her the watch. "Not likely I'd know some wealthy diamond peddler. What about him?"

"He was murdered last night in his New York hotel room."

"That's a tough way to go."

"The young woman who was in charge of scheduling and planning his New York exhibitions has disappeared, along with jewelry valued at two hundred and twenty-five million dollars."

"So she killed him, stole the jewels and went on the run. It's about what you'd expect these days. Can't trust those big-city people. So what does this have to do with me?"

"The name of the young woman who disappeared is Jade Dalton."

His stomach knotted. "Not *my* Jade?"

"Take a look for yourself." She opened the envelope, pulled some folded sheets of paper from it and handed them to him.

He glanced at the headline of the printed article:

Famed Jeweler Murdered in New York Hotel.

A picture of Quaid Vaquero and an article followed. Jade Dalton's name jumped out at him.

"Where did you get this?"

"Off the internet," Carolina said. "I was checking the national news while I drank my coffee. There's a picture of Jade on the next page."

R.J.'s throat dried up so fast he couldn't swallow as he stared at the photo. It had been almost two years since his daughter showed up right here on the Dry Gulch Ranch for the reading of his will. He'd forgotten a lot of things. Jade wasn't one of them.

His hands shook and he felt as if he was getting ready to lose his breakfast.

"It's my Jade, all right."

"I hated to tell you this, but I thought you'd want to know."

"Damn straight I want to know." He shook his head. "It's just hard to get my mind around this. Jade—a murderer. If she killed him, she must have had a very good reason."

"Two hundred million dollars plus is a lot of reasons," Carolina reminded him.

"Nope. I'm not buying that Jade would kill for money. Not after she let me know in no uncertain terms she wasn't interested in inheriting any of mine."

"Your will had rigid stipulations," Carolina said. "But the facts aren't in. There's no proof Jade had anything to do with the murder. She might be frightened and on the run or…" Carolina hesitated.

"Or in the hands of the real killer or worse," R.J. finished the sentence for her.

"Do you know how to get in touch with Jade's mother?" Carolina asked.

"Not a clue. Woman's last name changes more often than Texas weather. But I figure Travis can find out what this is all about. It pays sometimes to have a son who's a Dallas homicide detective."

Sure as shootin', Jade wouldn't be calling R.J. or running to him for help.

So it was up to him to find her. He would, even if it meant hiring every private detective in New York. He just prayed it wouldn't be too late.

Chapter Three

Booker Knox woke alone in a hotel bed that felt as if he'd landed on a fluffy cloud. After a year of back-to-back special missions as a Navy SEAL in the Middle East, he'd almost forgotten what a real bed felt like.

Still half-asleep and loving the feeling, he staggered to the bathroom in the nude, took a leak and then washed his face and hands. The man who stared back at him from the mirror looked years older than Booker felt and definitely needed a shave.

But that could wait until later, he decided, after he soaked up some more luxury in the good old US of A. He grabbed the room-service menu on his way back to bed. What he needed now was coffee, hot, black and strong.

He ordered a large pot of brew, steak, two eggs over easy and biscuits with gravy. "Double gravy," he told the operator. "And grits if you have them." He couldn't remember the last time he'd had grits. Not that the California version would be like what his grandma used to make.

"A side of grits. Will there be anything else for you?"

"That should do it for now."

"It should be in your room in about thirty minutes."

"That will work." Give him plenty of time to decide what he wanted to do with his first full day back in the

States. First on the list was slip into a pair of clean jeans so that he didn't flash the room-service attendant.

Now that he thought about it, tugging on his jeans might be the only thing he did today. He'd turn on the TV and catch some movies on the tube. Surely something worth watching had been released over the past year.

All he asked for was story lines with nothing to do with wars or death or blowing up buildings. Which left him with chick flicks. He could handle that if the starlets were hot.

Which would no doubt make him even hungrier for a real live woman. Good-looking. Fun-loving. Temporary.

In thirty days, he'd be back on the job and he wasn't about to try to manage a relationship and his SEAL duties. A lot of men could, but it wasn't for him.

He stood, walked over to the window, opened the curtains and looked out on the California coastline. A more gorgeous view would be hard to find. He might just spend his whole leave here. Generally he'd have taken a few days to slide back into normalcy and then gone to visit his parents.

But that was when home would have felt like home. It wouldn't now that his mother had died. He and his father had never gotten along particularly well. Things would be even more strained between them without his mother's warmth and enthusiasm for life to smooth the tension.

And now his sister Sylvie was dead, as well. Killed on the streets of Houston, Texas, when she'd been mistaken for her twin sister, Brit Garner Dalton.

The sister Booker had never heard of until she'd called him with the bad news. Talk about family skeletons shaking out of the closet. Who knew his mother had hidden such a scandalous past?

He had talked to Brit a few times since then. Short

conversations since she was busy raising Sylvie's baby girl, Kimmie. Brit seemed nice enough and she'd invited him more than once to visit her on the ranch that belonged to her new husband's father.

Booker wasn't much in the mood for taking on a new family, but he would like to meet his niece. He figured he kind of owed that to his mother and his dead half sister. Kimmie was seven months old now. He had no idea what a seven-month-old was like.

He hated to admit it, but the even bigger draw might be the Dry Gulch Ranch, just outside Dallas. Weather should be nice there in May. Perfect for climbing into a saddle. It was at least five years since he'd ridden. He'd missed it.

Missed his grandparents and the Oklahoma ranch that had been barely big enough to keep up a few head of cattle and a couple of horses. Booker had spent the best summers of his life on that ranch.

According to Brit, the Dry Gulch had over five hundred head of cattle grazing in the pastures and two horse barns.

Riding an open range on a spirited filly might be exactly the kind of R & R he needed. Besides, if he hated it there or found the whole experience of forging new family ties too awkward, all he had to do was ride off into the sunset like an old-time cowboy.

He should probably call first, let Brit know he was taking her up on her invitation. On the other hand, he might change his mind about visiting before he got there, so better just to surprise her. He'd call after breakfast and book a flight for tomorrow or the next day—if he could find one that didn't cost more than his budget would stretch.

He picked up the remote, turned on the TV and then pulled on his jeans. He surfed until he landed on a cable news channel. A gorgeous blonde was smiling at him while she described a developing murder case—the victim a famous jewelry designer in the United States from Spain.

They flashed a picture of a woman they referred to as a person of interest. Wow. Talk about hot. The Spanish dude should have known to avoid her. A woman that sexy was always trouble.

Exactly the kind of woman he was *not* looking for and not likely to find on the Dry Gulch Ranch.

Jade Dalton. The same last name as Brit now that she'd married Kimmie's daddy, Cannon. Could there possibly be a connection?

Naw. No way. There had to be thousands of Daltons in the country.

He went back to surfing channels and thinking about the Dry Gulch Ranch. The more he thought about it, the better it sounded.

Back in the saddle, wind in his face, a fishing pole in his hand. And not even a hint of danger in the air.

Chapter Four

Jade forced herself from the throes of the terrifying nightmare and opened her eyes. The room was shadowed. Unfamiliar. Cluttered. Pungent odors of stale cigarette smoke, beer and spicy food made her stomach roll.

The nightmare returned in full force. The vertigo. The loud voices. The gun. Needles poked into her arm.

For a second she thought she might be dead. But death didn't include pain and she had a killer headache along with a punishing thirst and need to rinse a sickening metallic taste from her mouth.

Kicking off the dingy sheet, she shuddered as she slid her feet to the floor. Her feet were bare, but she was still wearing the red cocktail dress she'd worn last night. One strap was broken. Dried blood painted a weird-shaped stain down the front of it. Apparently the blood wasn't hers, but it likely attributed to the disgusting odor.

She looked up as a door creaked open.

"Good. You're awake. Maybe now you'll start talking sense."

She turned and stared into the face of Reggie Lassiter. Relief surged through her. If she was with Reggie, she must be safe.

She looked around the room again, recognizing nothing but sure she wasn't in a hospital. "Where are we?"

"We're outside the city, just before the falling-off place on the edge of nowhere."

"Why? What happened?"

"You don't remember?"

"Not much. I was in Quaid's hotel suite. He was showing me the necklace that would highlight his showing. I got sick. The rest is confusing."

"You must remember something."

"There were voices, men I don't know. And you. You were there. I remember that. You must know what happened."

"From what I hear, that necklace must be a nice little bauble. It would make a sweet nest egg, or so I hear."

The sarcasm scratched along her raw nerves. She studied Reggie. Unlike her, he was dressed neatly in jeans and a blue sport shirt, hair combed, freshly shaved. He looked like the competent police officer she'd worked with before, but he definitely didn't sound like that man.

"What's going on? Where's Quaid," she demanded.

Reggie smirked as if she'd made a bad joke. "Quaid is gone to a better place and I'm not talking about Barcelona."

"Not dead. Tell me you don't mean he's dead."

"Afraid so."

"How? Who killed him?"

"Doesn't really matter. You're the one you should be worried about now."

"What do you mean?"

"Because if you don't tell me where you and Quaid hid that necklace in the next five minutes, you'll be joining your phony Spanish jewelry god."

Impulsively, her hand flew to her neck. It was bare, as she should have known it would be. "You think I took the necklace?"

"I know you didn't take it. You left with me, sweetheart. The necklace is not on your body and it wasn't on Quaid's. But it was around your pretty little neck before I arrived on the scene."

"Were you spying on Quaid? Was his suite bugged?"

"Not that I know of."

"Then how do you know I tried on the necklace?"

"You were wearing it when room service delivered Quaid's champagne."

The costly necklace was missing and Reggie had brought her here to search and intimidate her as if she were a common criminal. "Is this how the police work now? Threats? Intimidation? False accusations?"

"Not threats, Jade. Promises. The clock is ticking. Unless you want to pay your lover Quaid a surprise visit, you'd best start talking."

Reality finally seeped through the brain fog. Whatever had happened last night, Reggie was in on it, possibly the mastermind, though there had been others.

"A dirty cop. You disappoint me, Reggie. I expected so much more of you."

"No, like you, I'm just after what I can get in the world, only I don't have your looks to sleep my way into wealth."

Ire rose in her throat. She struggled to keep control. This was no time to go off half-cocked. She had a lot more to worry about now than defending her morals.

"The last I remember, the necklace was still around my neck. If anyone took it, it had to be you or one of your partners in crime."

"Wrong answer."

Jade stared into Reggie's eyes and shuddered at the icy threat she saw reflected in them. The lines of his face were drawn into sharp angles. His muscles clenched.

He pulled a pistol from his shoulder holster and pointed it at her head. "Either the necklace or a bullet, Jade. Now."

Her blood ran cold. He was not merely threatening. He meant to kill her if she didn't tell him how or where to find the missing jewelry. A location she couldn't possibly reveal since she had no idea where it was.

There had to be a way out of this. She just had to find it. Quick. She put her fingers to her temples. "I can't think clearly. It's all the drugs you pumped into me. I need time for my mind to clear."

"Then I guess you'd better get used to your surroundings. I can't sit around and make chitchat all day. I have to get back on the job."

"Playing the role of good cop?"

"Yeah. All those years of bit roles in bad TV shows before joining the force are finally paying off. The chief gave me a new assignment this morning—to find the sexy event planner who killed Quaid Vaquero and disappeared with his multimillion-dollar masterpiece."

So Reggie had not only killed Quaid but found a way to blame it on her. And once he got his hands on the necklace he'd kill her, too. He was way too smart to leave any loose ends to foul up his scheme.

Even if she convinced him she didn't know the whereabouts of the necklace, he'd kill her.

"If you know I was wearing the necklace, the champagne delivery must have been part of your scheme," she said, buying time.

"Absolutely. A nice touch, don't you think? A little Rohypnol for you and Quaid to make our encounter so much more pleasant for everyone. Also convenient that you were so enthralled with Quaid that you didn't notice the drug being slipped into your newly uncorked bottle of bubbly."

"You cops do think of everything."

Which would make outsmarting him difficult. She looked around the room again, this time searching for anything she could use as a weapon or an escape route.

There was only one door, the one Reggie had entered through and closed behind him so that she couldn't see past this one room. The two small windows on the other side of the bed were shuttered, no doubt nailed shut from the outside.

The clutter in the room consisted of piles of old magazines and newspapers, stacks of cardboard boxes that had been secured with heavy tape, several fishing rods, an empty cigarette pack and an open box of shotgun shells. No sign of a shotgun.

Her black evening handbag was on a marred pine table, its few contents scattered around it, including her wallet. Her stilettos were on the floor. Used just right, they could put an eye out, though she couldn't imagine them being a match for Reggie's ready pistol.

Inches of dust had accumulated on everything. Brown stains spread over the ceiling where water had leaked through.

"Where are we?" Jade asked.

"My late father's fishing camp. It was about all he left me and my brother."

"In New York?"

"Yes, but miles from the city. Feel free to scream for help. No one will hear you."

"I suppose your brother, Mack, is in on this, too."

"Nope. Mack is a stickler for rules. Doesn't even get parking tickets. Always was Dad's favorite. Still is Mom's."

"I wonder why."

Mack Lassiter owned and operated the security company that Ruth Stevens, Jade's boss at Effacy Corporate Event Planning, always insisted they use. At least it was nice to know Mack was honest, even if his moonlighting brother was evil to the core.

Mack would surely know about the fishing cabin. Only there was no reason he'd come looking for her, no reason for him to suspect his cop brother was involved in Quaid's murder or in her disappearance.

For all Jade knew, the other men in the hotel room last night were also cops, possibly even working the security detail with Reggie.

If she managed to escape, did she dare call the police for protection or would that just guarantee that Reggie would be the first to reach her?

"What am I supposed to do for a bathroom?" she asked.

"There's an outhouse. You'll have to watch for spiders, rats and yellow jackets. They've pretty much taken over the place. And be on the lookout for roaches inside the pages of the old catalog that serves as tissue."

Her stomach retched. Still she straightened her dress as best she could, wishing she'd worn something that buttoned to the neck—not that she owned any dresses like that.

"Bring it on," she said, going for fake bravado. She could do without the outhouse, but she did need to see what was outside this room and to search for an escape route.

"Actually, we have indoor plumbing these days," Reggie admitted. "But I don't advise drinking or even washing your mouth out with it. Pipes are rusted."

He walked over to the door and opened it, then motioned for her to lead the way. "Almost forgot," he taunted, just as she reached the door. "I have a bracelet for you, though not nearly as becoming as the earrings your Spanish lover gave you."

So he knew about not only the necklace but the earrings as well, information she hadn't had until minutes before the champagne arrived.

Reggie obviously had an accomplice on the inside. But who? The only employee Quaid had brought to the States was Javier Aranda, a longtime friend who had come two weeks before Quaid's arrival to check out the hotel where Quaid had reservations and to meet with Ruth and Jade. Javier had left to fly back to Barcelona a few days after Quaid's arrival.

Reggie slipped the handcuffs around her wrist and locked them. "That way," he said, shoving her past him.

The bathroom was down a short, narrow hallway. Just past that she glimpsed a large square room with a range, a refrigerator and a dinette set, all old and worn enough that they'd feel at home in the Smithsonian.

Reggie shoved her again, this time into the bathroom. "The door stays open a crack," he said. He took out his gun and waved it around threateningly before stepping away and leaving her alone.

He wasn't taking any chances with her escaping, but he wasn't going to shoot her, not as long as he thought she knew the location of the costly necklace. That was the one thing in her favor.

Inhibited by the cuffs, she struggled to get her panties down and take care of business. As she pulled them up again, Reggie's words came back to haunt her. He'd searched her for the necklace, and that obviously involved more than just patting her down.

There was no mirror, so she pulled up her dress and examined her body as best she could. No bruises around her thighs, breasts or abdomen, though there was a nasty one on her left arm. No bite marks around her nipples. No pain inside her that would indicate rape.

Thankfully, Reggie was apparently too obsessed with finding the necklace to concern himself with anything else. As bad as things were, they could have been worse. She'd hold on to that and take it as a good omen.

A quick look around the bathroom revealed nothing but soap, a damp hand towel on a hook and a dead cockroach.

No blades. No scissors. No bottles or mirrors she could break into a shard of jagged glass. She lingered at the stained sink, letting the lukewarm water splash over her hands as she soaped them repeatedly. Slowly a plan began to form in her mind. Risky, but it beat certain death by a mile.

She shook her hands to dry them rather than use the dirty towel. Fear gnawed at her stomach like claws, but she refused to give in to it. She clenched her teeth and forced a steady breath as she prepared to face Reggie with her lies.

He kicked open the bathroom door, sending it slamming against the bathroom wall. "You've stalled long enough, Jade." He peppered the demand with a stream of four-letter words.

Reggie handed her a bottle of water as she stepped out of the bathroom. She took it before he changed his mind. She drank half the bottle before he shoved her back toward the room that had become her prison.

Once inside, he kicked the door shut again.

"Where's the necklace, Jade?"

She sighed as if she'd lost the battle of wits. "How about a deal?"

"You don't have a bargaining tool."

"If you kill me without a deal, you have no necklace. And I can assure you that you won't find it on your own."

"What's the deal?" he asked.

"I'll go back to the hotel with you and show you where to find the necklace. We sell it on the black market as a team and I get half the profits."

He smirked as he pretended to be considering her offer. He'd agree, of course. Nothing to lose since even if she gave him the necklace, he'd kill her—unless she found a way to escape first. Her life literally depended on that.

"Once I have the necklace in hand, then we talk money. But you don't go with me. You're a killer on the run, remember? You tell me where to find the necklace. If it's not where you say it is, I kill you. Couldn't be much simpler than that."

"I go with you or no deal," she countered.

"How big a fool do you think I am? If someone spots us at that hotel together, we'll both be arrested."

"If you want the necklace, you do it my way." Her chances for escape would be much better in the city. "Get me the appropriate clothes and shoes and a wig. I'll go in disguise. If someone from the hotel sees me, they'll assume I'm a fellow detective."

"Do you really think I'd trust you to go back to the scene of the crime and not alert someone what was going on?"

"You will if you want the necklace that you've already killed for. Fifty-fifty, partner."

Reggie clenched his fist and looked as if he might be about to plant it in her face. Instead, he spit out a stream of curses.

"A dark-colored wig and not the cheapest one you can find," Jade specified. "They scream fake. Pants and shirt, size six. Shoes, size seven. Something comfortable." That she could run in. "And a toothbrush and toothpaste so that my foul-smelling breath doesn't stink up the lobby."

"You won't be in the lobby."

But he didn't say she wouldn't be going to the hotel. This could work.

"I'll think about it," he said. "But if you double-cross me…" He pulled his gun again and let it do the rest of his talking for him.

She didn't need the reminder. She'd come up with a plan to buy time and perhaps get back into the city. Now she needed a plan to stay alive.

"I'll be back soon," Reggie said. "In the meantime, think about your poor dead Spanish lover and know if you make one wrong move, you'll be joining him at the morgue."

"Quaid wasn't my lover."

"Why not? Weren't you good enough for him?"

Reggie opened the bedroom door, then looked back at her with a stupid smirk on his face. "Oops, almost forgot. I shouldn't leave you locked up this way." He took out a key, loosened the cuff on her left wrist and then dragged her back to the bed.

This time the bastard fastened one link around the iron headboard before relocking the cuffs.

He laughed as he swaggered to the door. "Enjoy yourself, darling. I'll be back in an hour or two."

FURY ERUPTED AND Jade stamped her foot so hard the old floorboards groaned. Enough energy wasted on useless rage, she decided quickly. Handcuffs and heavy iron bedstead notwithstanding, she was alone for an extended period of time. This might be her best—or only—opportunity to come out of this alive.

If something happened to Reggie while he was gone, and she couldn't unlock the handcuffs, she could die of thirst out here or be bitten by spiders or stinging scorpions. Who knew what crept around this place?

She forced the creepy thoughts aside. She had to think rationally.

Fortunately, she was not totally without skills. Ex-stepfather number four had been a Los Angeles Special Crimes Unit detective. He'd taught her a thing or two about self-defense and handcuffs.

Most handcuffs could be unlocked without a key. At least that was true a few years back. He'd shown her how one night when they were watching *Law and Order* together. He'd loved crime shows. Watching them let him point out all the inconsistencies between TV investigations and real ones.

He'd used a hairpin, but something else might work. If she could get close enough to reach the table where the contents of her sequined handbag had been dumped, she might find a suitable substitute.

She tugged hard. The bed didn't budge. She needed something to provide some leverage. She pushed her right foot hard against the wall and tugged again. This time the bed frame scooted at least an inch.

That was a start, but she'd have to move it at least three feet to reach the table. She tugged again. More movement.

After what seemed an eternity of working to the accompaniment of thunder rumbling ominously in the background, she stopped to catch her breath and give her aching back a rest.

When she dropped to the bed, she glimpsed the tip of what looked like a knife blade. She jumped off the bed and got down onto the dirty floor on her hands and knees for a better look.

Sure enough, there was some kind of knife under the bed. Not a kitchen knife but the kind used in hunting or fishing. Ex-stepfather number two had done both.

She went back to tugging on the bed. A few more inches and she was able to reach the knife.

Heart pounding, she picked it up and examined it. The blade was rusted and dust bunnies had cuddled up to it and the handle. Still, it might work.

She dropped back to the bed and tried to remember exactly how number four had taught her to pick the lock. Holding the edge of the faded sheet, she managed to swipe the point of the blade across it.

She had to work with her hands at a weird angle as she poked at the keyhole with the knife. The attempt was useless. The blade was too wide and thick to fit into the hole.

She needed something with a much smaller tip yet strong enough to push down on the part of the lock that made contact with the thingamajig.

Exasperated but no less determined, she laid the knife on the bed and went back to tugging the heavy bed frame across the wooden floor. When she finally reached the table and examined the scattered contents of her handbag, her frustration swelled. She saw absolutely nothing that might work.

Unwilling to give up, she reached into the sequined clutch and ran her fingers along the inside of the thin interior pocket and the folds in the lining at the bottom of the bag. The thumb of her left hand slid along what felt like a paper clip.

Tears wet her eyes and she pulled it out. This had to work. She had to make it work.

Jade had done this years ago with a hairpin. If she could do it then, she could surely do it now that her life was riding on success. She opened the clip as she'd been shown, bending it into an L-shape.

Once in place, she turned gently. Nothing moved except the paper clip.

She tried again, just the way number four had shown her, push and turn. This time her fingers slipped from the paper clip and it fell to the floor and bounced under the table.

Her nerves were frayed to the point of breaking. But she couldn't give up.

Down on her knees again, she spotted and retrieved the paper clip. This time she sat down on the bed and tried to calm her anxiety to the point her hands weren't trembling.

Nice and easy. Fit the end of the paper clip into the lock and firmly turn.

She squealed when the handcuffs clicked open. No worry. No one was around to hear.

Free from bondage. Jade's spirits rebounded, reviving her energy and her brain. She raked the items into her open handbag, picked up her shoes by the narrow straps and rushed to the door.

It was locked tight.

The bastard.

Grim determination took hold. She'd get out of here if she had to dig the door lock off with the dull knife. And then she'd probably find that he'd fit some kind of brace across the door to make sure she couldn't open it.

Think positive. Pray.

She did both as she went back for the paper clip. She looped the handbag's wristband and the shoes straps around the doorknob to free her hands as she worked on the lock.

A huge clap of thunder rattled the windows. A few seconds later, the lights went out, leaving the room in pitch-darkness. Even the weather was contriving against her. If she dropped the paper clip now, she might never find it.

The next clap of thunder sounded as if it was going to tear the house apart.

Jade took a deep breath. She had to do this. She had to get out of here. Using her fingers as a guide, she worked to fit the clip back into the lock. Her grip was tight and sure as she turned it in the lock.

Another clap of thunder.

No.

This time it wasn't thunder. It was the slamming of a car door. Reggie was back. He'd be furious when he discovered she'd gotten out of the handcuffs. But not nearly as violent as he'd become when they reached the hotel and she couldn't produce the necklace.

Panic rushed through her in waves. Maybe someone else had found the necklace. Maybe he was back merely to kill her and there would be no other chance for escape.

The paper clip slipped from her fingers. She rushed back to the bed and grabbed the knife. She had to try something. She wasn't ready to die.

Stepping behind the door, she held the rusty-bladed knife over her head, poised to strike the second Reggie opened the door and stepped into the room.

One chance. One split-second chance to plunge the knife into the dirty cop's back and hope it at least slowed him down enough she could make a run for freedom.

The doorknob turned and someone stepped inside, letting in light from the hallway. Life or death. This was it.

Without being able to see a face, Jade struck, pushing the knife through clothes, skin and muscle with all the strength she could muster.

"You bitch." Reggie screamed a stream of vile curses.

She'd hit her mark, put the knife right between the shoulder blades, but not nearly as deep as she'd been going for.

Reggie didn't fall, but staggered a few steps and then grabbed on to the bedpost. Blood from the wound wet the back of his shirt and dripped down his trousers.

Jade didn't dare go for his car keys. With only her instincts for survival to rely on, she yanked her purse from the doorknob and took off running. She tripped over an open duffel that had been left on the floor between the kitchen table and a filthy orange sofa. Somehow she managed to stay upright.

By the time she reached the front door, she could hear Reggie's footsteps behind her, slower than normal but still coming.

She yanked open the front door. The rain was pouring from an almost black sky. But there on a table right near the door was a large shopping bag and a dingy gray raincoat, dripping wet but with Reggie's keys dangling from the pocket.

She grabbed the bag and the keys without stopping. Now, if his car would only start and not crank uselessly the way it always happened in horror movies.

She looked back as she climbed into the car. Reggie was still coming, his gait like a drunken Frankenstein's, his eyes glazed like a madman's.

She slipped the keys into the ignition and the beautiful hum of an engine met her ears. She drove away in the storm, having no idea where she'd go.

She had to think this through, had to go somewhere she could slow down and regroup. Somewhere far away from New York where the media was surely playing up the story of Quaid's murder and splashing her picture all over newspapers and TV.

She needed to head for the last place anyone would expect her to show up.

Only one possibility came to mind.

A place with cows and mosquitoes, wasps and skunks—the four-legged kind. And rattlesnakes and big, hairy spiders. Her mother had told her about those.

The Dry Gulch Ranch, home of R.J. Dalton—her dear old dad.

He'd never been much of a father before. This would be his chance to shine.

Chapter Five

Two days and a lifetime of fear and anxiety later, Jade stepped off a plane at the Dallas/Fort Worth International Airport. She'd boarded the flight with trepidation, sure any second someone would recognize her in spite of her horrid wig and fake ID.

Even after she'd taken her seat and the plane had lifted into the air, she'd worried that somehow Reggie had tracked her and would be waiting when she approached the gate. After all, he had all the power and authority of the NYPD behind him.

She'd come close to calling the police herself, but whenever she did, she remembered the look on Reggie's face when he'd come after her, a trail of blood behind him.

Dread all but paralyzed her and she stopped halfway through the Jetway. People pulling luggage and shouldering bulky backpacks jostled her as they maneuvered past. She didn't move until the passengers had all exited and the flight attendants were walking toward her.

Finally she started walking again. Relief surged through her as she stepped into the gate area. No one was waiting for her. No one even gave her a second look. She checked the signs and started in the direction of baggage claim and ground transportation.

When she'd flown to Dallas almost two years ago, she rented a car and drove to the Dry Gulch Ranch. This time she was out of cash. The plane ticket had taken the last of the money in her wallet and she didn't dare use the ATM for fear Reggie was having it monitored.

She could probably take a taxi and let R.J. pay once she reached the Dry Gulch. Or she could risk hitchhiking as she'd done from New York to Atlanta, catching rides with truckers from one town and truck stop to the next.

But it was already after 7:00 p.m. and she was stressed to the breaking point. Climbing in another 18-wheeler with a stranger would surely push her over the edge. All she wanted was a safe place to close her eyes and sleep.

Following a stream of passengers, she crowded onto the escalator, her only luggage the shopping bag that held her strappy heels a toothbrush and toothpaste.

She was wearing the hideous black wig, a pair of black-rimmed glasses, the shoes and the shirt and jeans she'd found in Reggie's shopping bag.

The bloody dress was in a restroom at a truck stop back in Philly.

Once off the escalator, she started walking toward the taxi stop, still with no clear plan in mind. She spotted two men loitering next to that exit, both staring at her. Panic hit so swiftly she grew dizzy.

Struggling to calm herself with empty reassurances, she willed her feet to start walking in the opposite direction. Without slowing, she glanced over her shoulder. The men were only a few feet behind her and closing the space between them.

"Hey, lady," one of them called, waving to her.

She picked up her pace, practically running through the crowded airport. She turned a corner and ran smack into a man pulling a carry-on bag. He grabbed her arm to steady her.

She threw her arms around the man's neck and greeted him like a lover who'd just come home from a long war.

BOOKER STOOD THERE, too stunned to react to the stranger's kiss—for a half second. He figured the stranger had mistaken him for someone else, but that wasn't his fault. He threw himself into the kiss.

"I think you may have the wrong man, but I'm not complaining," he said when her lips left his.

"Play along with me," she said. "Act like we're together. I'll explain later."

"Works for me." What didn't work was the fear reflected in her gorgeous green eyes or the nervous way she kept glancing over her shoulder.

"I'm at your service. Is there someone here you need punched in the nose?"

"No. Start walking," she said, taking his arm.

"Where are we going?"

"To the taxi stand."

"How about we just walk over to the Avis counter? I have a car reserved. I'll drop you wherever you want to go."

"A ride would be great." She glanced over her shoulder again.

"Who is it you're trying to avoid?"

"No one."

"You're putting a lot of effort into this to avoid no one."

"I thought I saw my ex, but I was mistaken." She stopped walking and looked behind her, then let go of his arm. "You can go ahead with your plans. I'll be fine now."

She didn't sound fine. It didn't take a brain surgeon

to see that she was in trouble and running scared. Even if she hadn't been a fantastic kisser, he couldn't have walked away from that.

"Kiss and run is far worse than kiss and tell," he teased. "You should at least let me thank you for the spectacular welcome by giving you a ride."

"I'm going to Oak Grove. It's over an hour's drive from here."

"I've got nothing better to do." Not to mention that he was heading in that direction, anyway. "Do you have a name?"

Again, she hesitated way too long to be telling the truth. "Pam."

"Nice name." Just not hers, he'd wager.

"Mine's Booker Knox."

"Nice to meet you, Booker."

She stopped glancing over her shoulder as they made the short trek to the rental desk, but she didn't volunteer any additional information, either. Quiet. Mysterious. She had his curiosity aroused big-time.

Actually that kiss had aroused more than his curiosity.

Fifteen minutes later, they were in the rental and on the interstate. "Are you going to visit family?" he asked.

"Yes, but they live off the beaten path. There's a service station on the highway near Oak Grove. You can drop me off there. They'll come and pick me up."

"Are they expecting you?"

"Of course. They think I'm taking a taxi, but they'll be waiting for my call. What about you? Where are you going?"

"To a friend's ranch. My first time there, but from what I hear, it's a big spread with a rambling old house. I'm sure they can fit you in if you need a place to stay tonight."

"No, thanks."

"Are you from Oak Grove?" he asked.

"No."

"But you have family there."

"Yes."

"What's their name? I bet my friends know them. I hear it's a really small town."

"Smith."

Probably lying again. But why, unless she was worried about him being a pervert? "Am I making you uneasy?"

"A little. I don't normally accept rides from strangers."

Yet she'd kissed one in the airport. "Look, Pam, I can assure you I'm trustworthy. I'm a Navy SEAL on leave and in Oak Grove to visit my half sister. You can call her and she'll vouch for me."

She shook her head and pushed her ill-fitting glasses back up her nose. "That's not necessary."

But she was anxious about something, likely the same situation that had prompted the kiss. Possibly the ex-boyfriend she'd mentioned. Possibly not.

Traffic on the interstate was heavy. He figured the trip was going to take at least an hour and a half, and his stomach was already complaining that it was past dinnertime.

He took the next exit.

Pam, or whatever her name was, turned to face him. "Where are we going?"

"The freeway sign listed several fast-food choices at this exit. I'm starved. You must be, too, if you just got off a plane. A bag of peanuts and a sip or two of soda isn't very filling."

"I could use a bite."

"What's your choice?" he asked as they pulled off the frontage road and were confronted with a buffet of choices. "Burgers, tacos, fried chicken, barbecue?"

"You pick."

"It all looks good to me. There was a severe shortage of artery-clogging fast-food joints in the mountainous wilds of Afghanistan." He pulled into a familiar chain where he knew the burgers were good and the strawberry shakes even better.

He parked and they went inside. "Nothing like the smell of a burger on the grill." He ordered two half pounders, fries and a large shake. She ordered a salad.

"Kind of defeats the purpose of going to a greasy-food joint if you eat healthy," he said, hoping a little teasing would help her loosen up enough to talk about what was really going on with her.

"I need to go wash up," she said.

Booker watched her walk away. Great butt in a pair of well-fitting jeans, but nothing about her quite rang true. Big-rimmed glasses that kept sliding down her nose as if they belonged to a big brother. The ugly black hair was a wig, a cheap one at that. The jeans were new. So was the T-shirt, as evidenced by the price tag hanging out the back of the neckline. New and several sizes too big.

His guess would be that she was running scared from something or someone.

On the run. Damn. What was he thinking?

Booker rushed to the door, almost knocking down a middle-aged woman who was entering as he was leaving. Just as he expected, Miss Mysterious had left through the back door and was already hightailing it down the road.

He jumped in the rental sedan and gunned the engine, sliding into rescue mode with only a minuscule of concern for the fact that he rescuing a woman who didn't want to be rescued.

He pulled the car to a stop on the shoulder a few feet in front of her. "Get in the car," he ordered.

She kept walking. Booker threw the gear into Park and jumped out of the rental. He walked over, grabbed her arm and tugged her to a stop.

"I don't take kindly to being stood up for dinner."

She met his gaze, her voice low but her eyes shooting fire. "Take your hands off me."

He did. That settled one thing. She wasn't running from an abusive lover. If that look was any indication, she'd have made mincemeat of a man who'd gotten out of line with her.

"I'm sorry," he said. "Let's start over. My hunch is you're in some kind of trouble, and my hunches are incredibly accurate. I'd like to help if I can or at least drop you off wherever it is you're heading. I don't like the idea of dropping you at a service station."

"Why?"

"Standing on the side of a road is dangerous."

"I mean, why are you so insistent on putting yourself out for me?"

"You're a good kisser."

"I'm serious, Booker. What's in this for you?"

"I'm the hero type."

She took a deep breath and exhaled slowly. "Okay. I don't need any help, but you can drive me to my friend's ranch—under two conditions."

"Shoot."

"No more questions. And once you drop me off, forget you ever saw me."

"If you wanted me to forget you, you should have started with a handshake instead of a kiss, but I'll give it my best shot."

"Then let's go back and pick up our food order. I really am starved."

"Finally, we agree on something." He went through

the drive-through and picked up their food after the hassle of explaining to the woman at the window why he'd changed his mind and now wanted his food to go.

He ate as he drove, spilling loose lettuce and a paper-thin slice of overripe tomato down his shirt. He kept his promise not to ask questions until they were about thirty minutes out of the city and traffic was finally moving smoothly.

"So, does this ranch we're going to have a name?"

"The Dry Gulch. Now, doesn't that sound inviting?"

He hadn't been ready for that shocker, but suddenly the facts came together. The woman sitting next to him was wearing a wig and what she was running from was the law.

He was now harboring a fugitive from justice, a fugitive whose crime had the entire country and half of Europe up in arms.

But damn, could Jade Dalton kiss!

JADE FELT THE tension grow with each mile they got closer to the Dry Gulch Ranch. Her problems were far from over. The NYPD surely had a warrant out for her arrest by now. She could possibly put off facing them for another day, but facing R.J. and the rest of the Daltons was imminent.

It was difficult to imagine that any of the Daltons would be glad to see her and the pack of trouble she brought with her. They might even call the local sheriff and have her arrested tonight.

It was a chance she had to take.

"I'll get the gate," she said when Booker stopped at the entrance to the ranch.

She breathed deeply, filling her lungs with the fresh country air. The smells were different here. So were the sounds. Wind whispering through the branches high atop the towering pines. Loud chirping from crickets or perhaps the tiny tree frogs she'd heard about on her last trip to the ranch.

The croak of a bullfrog. The lonesome hoot of an owl. A rustle in the nearby grass that sent her rushing back to the car the second she'd closed the gate behind them.

"Nice spread," Booker said as they drove past acres of fenced pastureland, "at least what I see of it in the moonlight."

"If you like living on the outskirts of civilization."

"I take it you don't."

"I'm a big-city girl. The bigger the better."

"Where do you live?"

"There you go with the questions again."

"Sorry about that."

Fortunately, he drove the rest of the way in silence, throwing on the brakes once to avoid hitting a deer that dashed across the road just a few yards in front of them.

The rambling ranch house sneaked up on them, the lights from the windows peeking at them from between tree branches as they rounded a curve in the ranch road.

"Looks like they left the lights on for you," Booker said.

"I'm surprised they're not all in bed by now."

"It's only eight-thirty."

"But what else is there to do out here when the sun goes down."

"Watch TV. Read a book. Chat on Facebook. I've heard some people even engage in conversation if they're really desperate."

Booker pulled into the wide driveway and for a second, Jade thought they were at the wrong house. It looked better cared for than she remembered it. Of course, that

might be because she was seeing the place in the cover of darkness instead of the bright glare of daylight.

"I can take it from here," she said as Booker killed the engine.

"I always walk my dates to the door."

"We're not on a date." He'd be peeling out and squealing tires in his rush to get away if he knew the truth about her.

"Thanks for the ride," she said. "Enjoy your leave."

"I have a hunch it won't be boring."

Ignoring her assurance that she no longer needed him, he got out of the car and followed her up the walk.

An attractive blonde opened the door before they reached it. "Finally we meet," she said. "I'm Brit and you must be Booker."

"In the flesh." Booker put out a hand, but the woman pulled him into a hug, totally ignoring Jade.

Apprehension skidded along her nerve endings. Had she been set up? Had Booker been looking for her at the airport when she ran into him and saved him the trouble?

No wonder he chased after her when she sneaked off from the burger joint.

Booker stood back and studied the woman who'd just embraced him so warmly. "Excuse me, but this is going to take a minute for me to get past. You look exactly like Sylvie."

"I thought I'd prepared you for that," she said, "but I guess nothing really could."

"No. I'll get used to it, but it's a shocker now."

Jade stood there, flabbergasted. She had no idea what was going on, but apparently Booker's coming here had nothing to do with her.

"You must be a friend of Booker's," Brit said, directing her comment to Jade.

A friend of Booker's. That was an intriguing mistake. If she could pull that off, it would definitely simplify matters. It would give Jade a chance to think things through tonight before confronting the Daltons.

"Yes, Booker and I are—"

Her sentence was interrupted by the sound of approaching footfalls. She looked up as R.J. shuffled to the door. The lie died on her lips.

He looked years older than he had the last time she'd seen him. Frailer, his stance less intimidating, his hair gray wisps that barely covered his head. The inoperable tumor hadn't killed him yet, but it was apparently taking its toll.

He stared at her, his mouth open, his eyes wide.

"Jade." His voice broke on her name.

So much for her disguise. If R.J. could recognize her that easily, she'd fool no one who was actually looking for her. It was a miracle she'd made it to Dallas without being arrested.

"Thank God you're here," R.J. said. "I've been worried sick. I was about to hire a team of private detectives to track you down."

Coming here had clearly been a mistake. "I didn't kill anyone."

"I know that. I told everyone that as soon as we heard. I just wanted to find you and make sure you were safe."

"I was kidnapped. When I escaped, I didn't know anything else to do but come here. But I won't stay more than one night. I'll leave tomorrow morning, before I cause you any trouble."

"Of course you'll stay. Where else would you go? You're family."

"But you will have to turn yourself in to the local sheriff," Brit said. "And you'll need a lawyer."

"We've got the best danged attorney in the state of Texas right here on the ranch," R.J. interrupted. "Your half brother Leif. We'll call him right now. He'll know exactly how to handle this."

"He may not want to represent me."

"He's obliged. We Daltons stick together. His brother Travis will advise you, too. He's a Dallas homicide detective, and Brit here was a detective in Houston before she and Cannon got hitched. Everything you need is right here."

A lawyer and two homicide detectives. Jade would probably be in jail by morning.

"C'mon in," R.J. said. "You and your friend, afore the skeeters start snacking on you."

"This is Booker Knox," Brit said, introducing him to R.J. before things got any more confusing.

"Well, I'll be jiggered! You and Jade knowing each other. Don't that beat all?"

"Pretty surprising, isn't it?" Booker said, going along with everything.

"You two need something to eat? I can rustle up some leftovers."

"We had dinner in town," Jade said. "And Booker and I don't actually know each other," she added, determined to clear up that minor detail before they got bogged down even further in chaotic confusion. "We ran into each other in the car rental line at the airport and realized we were both coming to the same place." The partial truth would do.

"Well, that was damn lucky," R.J. said. "If your belly's full, how about a beer or a glass of wine while you two relax a bit? After that, Jade can bring Brit and me up to snuff on what really happened in that New York hotel suite."

"I could use a few minutes to freshen up," Jade said.

And to pull off the useless wig that was starting to feel like a wad of wet wool on her head before she faced the family firing squad. She couldn't imagine they'd all be as accommodating as R.J.

"Why don't I show you to the guest rooms," Brit offered. "Do you have luggage?"

"Afraid not," Jade said.

"I can lend you a clean T-shirt to sleep in," Booker said. "I'll get my bag out of the car."

"I'll put you in the room I prepared for Booker," Brit said as Booker left to go back to the car. "It has a private bath already stocked with the essentials like soap, shampoo, conditioner, lotions, toothpaste, razors, even extra toothbrushes in the top drawer if you need one."

"I appreciate that." Hopefully that meant they didn't intend to call the local sheriff out for an immediate arrest.

"We're about the same size," Brit said. "I'm sure I have a nightshirt and some jeans and shirts you can wear until you have time to shop. I'll gather up a few items while you get yourself together."

"Thanks. I'm sorry I came crashing in on R.J. and the rest of you like this. I panicked. That's the only excuse for going on the run the way I did."

"Don't apologize for coming here," Brit said. "R.J. was right. We're family. That's where you go when you're in trouble."

A nice concept, but it hadn't been Jade's experience. But she definitely needed to get in touch with her mother and let her know she was safe. Kiki would have heard the media's version of what had happened and she'd be bordering on hysteria about now. And no doubt full of advice as to how Jade should be handling this.

"R.J.'s been a wreck ever since we first heard about Quaid Vaquero's murder. He was afraid that you'd been murdered as well, and the police weren't releasing that information."

"I came close," Jade said, not expecting Brit to believe her.

"Whatever happened, you're safe now," Brit said. "So let's get you settled in. The only available guest rooms are upstairs. Cannon, Kimmie and I pretty much took over the first floor when we moved in. Someone needs to be close by, now that R.J.'s health is failing so fast."

Once Jade was alone in the guest room, her strained willpower caved like a sand castle in the rain. She dropped to the bed as the events of the past two days stormed her mind. The handcuffs. The iron bed. The pitch-black prison when the power had gone out.

Reggie, bloody, the eyes of a madman, chasing her as she fled from his brutal captivity.

It seemed unreal, a nightmare. But those were the truths she had to share with these strangers who posed as family.

Once she did, would they believe that she had no part in Quaid's murder and no idea what had happened to the necklace that had started this roller-coaster ride of terror?

Would anyone?

Chapter Six

Booker hadn't been exactly invited to join the family confab at the huge, marred farmhouse table that looked as if it had seen years of gatherings. It was more as though he'd pushed his way in and they had all been too polite to shove him away.

He was the outsider and yet from all indications, it seemed he knew Jade as well as or better than the official Daltons, including R.J.

He didn't intend to interfere unless he figured it was in Jade's best interest. Right now he was leaning to her side of the equation, but that could change in an instant if he became convinced she had anything to do with the murder or stealing the necklace.

The more she told them about the brutal kidnapping, the more she started to get to him. He admired her attitude.

Spunky. Fighting back against the murderous cop. Hitching her way from New York City to Atlanta when she seemed more the limo type.

Okay, why kid himself? It was also her looks that turned him on. Now that she'd shed the creepy wig and the black-rimmed glasses that looked as if they'd previously belonged to a giant mole, she looked almost exactly

like the photograph of her they'd flashed on TV back
when he was still in California.

On a scale of one to ten, he'd rank her a twelve, and
that was in the baggy T-shirt.

Hot and in danger. No SEAL worthy of his Trident
could resist that combo. He wasn't sure the rest of the
Daltons felt that same team spirit.

Booker had learned a little about the family dynam-
ics from Brit in their phone conversations over the past
four months. He'd learned a bit more from R.J. over a
beer while they waited for the others to begin to convene
for this meeting.

R.J. had lived his life estranged from his five sons
and Jade, most born of different mothers. Now that he
was living on borrowed time because of an inoperable
brain tumor, he was trying to make amends and get to
know them.

Booker had no idea how R.J. had persuaded four of
his six kids to move onto the Dry Gulch, but he figured
money had something to do with it.

Most of the Dalton clan was at the table now. Brit and
her husband, Cannon. Adam was there without his wife,
Hadley, who was home putting their twin four-year-old
daughters to bed.

Leif's very pregnant wife, Joni, was there, and Leif
was supposedly on his way from his Oak Grove law office. Travis and his wife, Faith, were in DC, where he
was taking part in a training session. That left Faith's
teenage son, Cornell, who was home studying for finals
in preparation for his graduation from high school next
week. And Leif's teenage daughter, Effie, by a previous
marriage, who was also home studying.

Jade was definitely outnumbered.

The back door opened and the man Booker assumed

was Leif stepped inside. "Sorry I'm late. I've got a major case wrapping up in court tomorrow and I had to make sure I'm ready for it."

They went through another round of introductions as Leif grabbed a beer from the fridge.

"Not to be rude," Leif said as he pulled up a chair. "But this is serious business. I know Jade has invited the entire family to be here—against my judgment, by the way—but I don't think it's wise for Booker to get involved."

"He's already involved," Jade said. "Nothing I say is going to change because he's sitting here."

"He may be forced to testify if this goes to trial."

"Not likely," Booker said. "I'll probably be half a world away by the time this goes to trial—not that I expect it to go to trial after hearing Jade's side of this."

"Let's just go with it," R.J. said. "Once we hear Jade out, I s'pect you'll know how to straighten everything out without her even going back to New York."

R.J. was a bit more optimistic than Booker. He studied the others sitting around the table. From their expressions, it was probably safe to say R.J. was a lot more optimistic than they were, as well.

Brit's husband, Cannon, rocked his empty beer bottle back and forth. "It was reported today that you were in Quaid's hotel suite when he was found murdered."

"That's quite possible. I'd been drugged, so my memories of that night are hazy."

"Do you remember seeing the missing necklace?" Brit asked.

"Yes. I had it on for a while. Quaid wanted me to wear it to the night's event, but I told him it wasn't safe, that it should be closely guarded at all times."

"Whoa," Leif ordered, taking control the way Booker had expected him to.

"I need to hear Jade's account from the beginning, without interruption. I can't begin to offer sound legal advice without knowing all the facts."

"Good idea," R.J. agreed. "And I'm sure I don't have to tell any of you that what goes on in this kitchen tonight had best not be bandied about outside this house."

"I'm sorry I dragged you all into this," Jade said. "I could just leave now and you could pretend you never saw me."

"Nonsense," Adam said. "You're not the first Dalton to bring trouble to the Dry Gulch and I'm sure you won't be the last. We pull together as a family."

"Okay, just remember you asked me to stay."

Everyone listened intently as Jade relayed what Booker figured was a shorthand version of what had transpired. He grew angrier by the second, so fired up that it was all he could do to sit there.

His insides clenched with the need to get his hands on Reggie Lassiter. He imagined pounding his fist into the son of a bitch's face until it was a pulverized mass of bloody flesh.

The heartless, brutal thug had killed Quaid Vaquero, then kidnapped Jade and put her through hell.

Amazingly, even that didn't crush her will to survive. Even with the dregs of Rohypnol still messing with her brain, her wrist handcuffed to an iron bed, locked and double-locked inside a cabin, she'd pulled off her own rescue.

The easy choice then would have been to call 911 at the first opportunity. Instead, she'd made decisions, taken risks, traveled out of Reggie's reach—at least for now.

Reggie had already killed for that necklace. He wasn't going to just cry uncle and give up his fortune because

Jade had escaped once. He'd keep coming after her until he had the necklace.

Or until one of them was dead.

But if Jade didn't have the necklace, who did?

Booker only half listened to the rest of Jade's story about hitching rides and buying a fake ID from some biker chick in a truck stop.

He'd faced more than his share of truly evil men over the past few years. They defied logic, thrived on hate, were obsessed with their own agenda.

Reggie Lassiter had all the markings of being that type of crazed lunatic.

Brit might believe the police would protect Jade. Maybe they could, maybe they couldn't—or wouldn't. But Booker could and would. He lived by the SEAL creed.

Failure was not an option.

Now all he had to do was convince Jade to turn her safety over to him. First he'd need a plan. With luck, he'd have the details worked out by morning.

EXHAUSTION LEFT JADE feeling like a zombie as she climbed the stairs to the guest bedroom. The fear that had driven her for the past two days had been replaced with muscle aches, anxiety and overwrought emotions.

Going over the details of the past two days in coherent order helped clear things in her mind, but the shock and grief had hit with renewed vengeance.

Three nights ago, Quaid Vaquero had been smiling, excited about the success of his visit to the States, incredibly proud of the beautiful diamond-and-emerald necklace he'd designed. He had his whole exciting life in front of him.

Now he was dead. If the necklace hadn't somehow

disappeared in the confusion, she'd be dead, too. If she hadn't been cuffed to that iron bed and found that dull-bladed fishing knife, she might still be imprisoned by a madman.

Now she was merely wanted by the NYPD for murder. And no doubt still being hunted by a killer. She wondered if he was still playing cop or if he'd walked off the job to chase her down, sure she had the necklace.

Booker followed her up the stairs a step behind. Oddly, she felt more connected to him than any of her half siblings.

"You've had a rough few days," Booker said when they reached the upstairs hallway. "You need a good night's sleep."

"In the worst way," Jade agreed.

"Have you even been to bed since you escaped the fishing camp?"

"I checked into a motel for a few hours last night, mostly to get a shower, but I dozed off. I didn't sleep long. It's difficult when you're expecting someone to bust through the door any second and take you prisoner again—or worse."

"You're safe now. Sleep sound tonight. I've got your back."

"Let this be a lesson to you, Booker Knox. Beware of women who sexually accost you in airports."

"Happens all the time," he teased. "I'm used to it."

"I'm still sorry I screwed up your reunion with Brit and Kimmie. Did you even get to see your niece?"

"Brit let me peek into the nursery where she was sleeping. The real test of my uncle prowess will come in the morning."

"If you're smart, you'll clear out after that and come back once I'm long gone, hopefully not to jail."

"Are you trying to get rid of me?"

"No way," she assured him, determined to keep the conversation light. "You're the only one here who's not a Dalton. That's a big plus in your column."

"So, how is it all your family are strangers?"

"By design."

"Your design?"

"Yes, but it's not personal," Jade said, "except where R.J.'s concerned. He was my ex-father even before I was born. According to my mother, he threw her out when she was barefoot and pregnant. Bear in mind, my mother is a drama queen, so that may not bear even the slightest resemblance to what really happened.

"As for my other five half siblings, I've only met them once, two years ago at the reading of R.J.'s will. We had one thing in common then. We all thought R.J. was nuts."

"The reading of the will while he was still alive. There must be a story there."

"Too long to get into tonight."

Jade leaned against her closed door and looked up and into Booker's mesmerizing stare. She was emotionally and physically drained, yet she wondered what it would be like to slip into his strong arms and hold on tight.

"Guess we should both get some sleep," she murmured.

"Yeah." But still he lingered. He trailed his fingers down her right arm and then took her hand in his. "If you need anything tonight, even just someone to talk to, all you have to do is call. I'm a very light sleeper. I'll hear you."

"Just knowing you're there will let me sleep a lot better. Thanks—for everything."

She turned, opened the door and stepped into her

room before she did something really foolish, like kiss him again.

Alone in her room, she stripped and stood under the hot spray of the shower for what seemed an eternity. When the tension in her nerves and muscles finally eased, she soaped the washcloth and scrubbed her body until the flesh hurt.

Even then, she felt dirty, soiled with Quaid's death and the evil she'd faced in the fishing camp. She pulled on the soft cotton nightshirt Brit had left for her and then slid between the crisp white sheets.

Shadows from the ceiling hypnotized her into a dull semiconsciousness as she drifted into sleep. Reggie was out there somewhere, but he couldn't get to her tonight.

Booker Knox had her back.

THE EXQUISITE JEWELS felt cold as they cascaded down Jade's naked skin and dipped into her cleavage. The jewels shimmered and then began to prick at her flesh like a million tiny insects. She tried to yank the necklace off.

Quaid grabbed her hands. "I insist you wear it for me, sweetheart."

"No, please. Get it off me."

She stared into the mirror. Quaid's eyes were like a blazing fire, but his face was deathly white, bones pushing through the pale flesh. Blood dripped from his lips as they brushed the back of her neck.

He let go of her hands and pulled her toward him. His body was as cold as the necklace. She began to shiver. He was still holding her tight, but he was dead. She had to get away. Run. Run anywhere. She pushed through the door.

Reggie was waiting for her. He yanked the necklace from her neck and then pushed her back into the hotel room and onto a macabre iron bed with teeth.

She tried to scream, but her throat closed, blocking the sound. She tried again and again. Nothing came out. And then there was a gnashing sound as the bed's mouth gaped open and began to suck her inside it.

Jade woke with a start. Her heart was pounding, her skin clammy. Her nightshirt was soaked with sweat. But there was no devilish bed and no Reggie.

Only a nightmare. She closed her eyes. When she opened them, she saw the shadowed man standing just inside her door.

She opened her mouth to scream.

"Are you okay?"

"Booker."

"Yeah. I heard noises. I wanted to make sure nothing was wrong."

"A nightmare," she said. "A bizarre, twisted contortion of what's been going on."

He walked over and sat down on the edge of the bed. "I'm not surprised. There are times the subconscious has to do the dirty work of releasing pent-up emotions."

"You sound as if you know that from experience."

"I do. I've seen things in the war zone that if I couldn't bury in my mind, I'd never be able to sleep. But tonight's not about me. Can I get you something? Warm milk? A hot toddy?"

"No. I'll be fine, as soon as my nerves settle down again." She tugged the damp nightshirt away from her skin.

"You need to change into something dry. My offer of a T-shirt still stands."

She looked down. Moonlight filtering through the window outlined her nipples against the wet nightshirt. Grabbing the hem of the sheet, she tugged it around her. "I accept the offer—if it's not too much trouble."

"No trouble at all, not that I was objecting to the view."

"Just get the shirt."

"Be right back."

Jade took a series of deep breaths as she watched him walk him away. Suddenly the scene seemed far too intimate. The moonlight, her in damp bedclothes, him wearing only a pair of jeans, zipped but not snapped. The fact that it was in the wee hours of the morning and that the nightmare had left her shaky and vulnerable didn't help any.

Worse was the growing attraction, totally implausible and inappropriate considering her angst-ridden situation. Or maybe the angst stimulated the attraction.

Booker took everything in stride. He hadn't so much as batted an eye when he discovered she was the now-infamous fugitive and suspected murderer.

He was appropriately serious when he should be and flirtatiously teasing when she needed that. Under other circumstances, they could have had a great time together.

She cut off her own thoughts before they strayed too far. Under ordinary circumstances, they would never have met. She'd have been in New York, not at the Dry Gulch Ranch.

As it was, she wouldn't be here long. She'd managed her own life since she was sixteen and her mother had married number five. She didn't need a family of strangers giving her orders now.

And there was certainly no point in dragging Booker Knox into this mess.

He returned with a neatly folded white T-shirt and tossed it onto the bed. He turned his back to her while she slipped into the shirt.

"I should go and let you get back to sleep?" he said, his voice rising as if it were more a question than a statement.

She didn't want him to leave, but she was not ready for what his staying might lead to.

"'To sleep, perchance to dream,'" she quoted. "Certainly not all it's cracked up to be."

"But a nightmare is only that, Jade. Reggie can't hurt you now without going through me. That's not going to happen."

It was an empty promise. Once she left the Dry Gulch Ranch and turned herself in to the police, everything would be out of her hands and Booker's.

Booker dropped into the easy chair by the window, tucked a throw pillow behind his head and parked his feet on the ottoman. "I'll stay here until you fall asleep. Wiggle any body part if you need me. I'll hear you."

"You don't have to do that."

"Don't tell a SEAL how to do his job. We're touchy about that."

"I'll keep that in mind," she said. She wasn't sure she'd fall asleep again, but her anxiety did ease having Booker nearby. She lay back, closed her eyes and started counting backward from one hundred.

She only made it to seventy-nine before sleep claimed her.

BOOKER WOKE AND STRETCHED. His stiff muscles and joints protested. He rubbed his neck and then noticed the first tint of sunrise outside the window. He'd obviously fallen asleep in Jade's chair. Her rhythmic breathing assured him she was still sleeping soundly.

He stood and tiptoed to the side of the bed. She'd curled up in the fetal position and her gorgeous auburn hair fanned the pillow.

Temptation swelled without warning and he imagined what it would feel like to crawl into bed beside her and spoon his body around hers. Imagined his hands curving around her soft breasts and the feel of his leg pressing between her thighs.

His body hardened and he walked away before she woke and found him staring at her. He went back to his room, raised the window and sucked in a gulp of air. It didn't fully erase the lust, but it helped.

It was mid-May and the stifling humidity of summer hadn't fully descended on North Texas yet. A breeze tickled new leaves and the early birds out for their worms sang as they worked. A hundred shades of green merged in the landscape. The smell of pine and heart scented the dew. A horse whinnied in the distance.

This was exactly the kind of much-needed break Booker had counted on when he'd decided to visit Brit at the ranch. What he hadn't counted on was Jade. Now she consumed his thoughts.

And the more he thought about her, the more convinced he was that she was still in danger and all the expertise and good intentions of her family might actually increase it.

He didn't fancy himself smarter, braver or more concerned than they were. But his training and experiences were definitely different. He looked at the worst that could happen and prepared for it.

With Jade, that left him only one option. Now he just had to convince the Daltons and Jade to go along with him.

The smell of coffee drifted up from the kitchen. Someone was up. He finished dressing and made his way downstairs. R.J. was standing at the open back door, staring out. His shoulders were stooped and part of his shirt was hanging out of his trousers.

"You're up early," Booker said.

"Don't have enough time left to go missing a morning like this one."

"Good. I thought maybe you were worrying about Jade and couldn't sleep."

"That, too." R.J. padded over to the counter. "Coffee's ready. You want a cup?"

"Love one," Booker said.

R.J. pulled two mugs from the shelf just over the coffeemaker. "There's cream in the fridge or the powdered kind in the jar with the red lid. The jar with the green lid's full for that fake sugar everyone uses these days."

"But not you?"

"I'm not going to live long enough to worry about my diet. Besides, I take my coffee black."

"Same here," Booker said.

"This time of the year, I usually have my first cup of coffee on the porch," R.J. said. "I'd welcome your company, but if you'd rather take yours and go out for a walk or back to your room, that's no problem."

"I'll join you on the porch," Booker said. "Actually, I have something to run by you and this is probably the best opportunity to do it."

"This something you want to talk about wouldn't have anything to do with Jade, would it?"

"As a matter of fact, it would."

"Good. All I could think about last night was that Reggie guy kidnapping and almost killing her. If I were a few years younger, I'd be out there trying to take care of that seven-sided SOB myself."

"I get that," Booker agreed.

"Yep, but since I can't go after him myself, I have to leave it to someone who can. I figure a SEAL should have some ideas for squashing that stinking cockroach."

Chapter Seven

R.J. liked Booker Knox. The guy didn't back away from trouble or confrontation. Here he was on leave, taking a break from war and up at dawn to tackle problems that weren't his responsibility.

That was the mark of a real man.

R.J. settled in his favorite rocker. Booker leaned against the porch railing. Big guy, R.J. noticed, not for the first time. Several inches over six feet. Didn't look like one those bodybuilders with the obscene muscles, but if he punched you solid, you'd be picking up yourself off the ground—if you could.

"What's your take on this, Booker?"

"First, I don't think rushing to the New York police is the way to proceed."

"Why not? Jade's innocent. There's no reason for her to avoid talking to the authorities. She can't put it off forever."

"I agree, but before she talks to them, we need to know what's going on that they're not releasing to the public."

"Such as?"

Booker looked up as Cannon joined them on the porch, coffee in hand, his jaw sporting a heavy coating of whiskers.

"What is it you need to know?" Cannon asked, having

obviously heard part of the conversation from inside the front door.

"I'd like to know what's going on with Reggie Lassiter for starters. Is he still on the job pretending to be a good cop or has he gone AWOL? Did he go to the hospital with his stabbing wound, and if he did, how did he say he got it?"

"Makes sense to me," Cannon said. "How do we find that out? Do you have connections with the NYPD?"

"No, but I figure Brit and Travis might be able to use their sources to get that information, hopefully without giving away any hints that they're in contact with Jade. If the media sharks get so much as a passing suspicion that she might be on the ranch, there'll be more of them around here than there are cows."

"That's the last thing we need," Cannon agreed.

"Nope," R.J. said, making sure they were all on the same page. "The last thing we need is for that varmint Reggie to get his hands on Jade again."

"In that case, it may be a bodyguard that she needs," Cannon said.

"She definitely needs a bodyguard," Booker said.

R.J. nodded. "Are you volunteering for the job?"

"I am."

"Have you talked to Jade about any of this?" Cannon asked.

"Not exactly. I promised her I had her back. I think we should just leave it at that until I find the opportune time to bring it up."

"Agreed," R.J. said. "You never know how a high-spirited, independent woman's going to react to needing a hero."

"But we can't leave the proposition of Jade's putting off turning herself in hanging in midair. So looks like we're in for another family meeting," Cannon said. "Good thing it's Saturday. Probably best to set it up right away before Leif and Brit talk to the NYPD. How about a sit-down right after breakfast?"

"I'm in," R.J. said.

The front door opened again, this time it was Brit holding a wiggling Kimmie in her arms. R.J. stole a kiss from his beautiful granddaughter and went back to the kitchen for more coffee.

It was time for Booker to meet his niece and he didn't need R.J. hanging around for that.

"THIS IS KIMMIE," Brit said, balancing the baby girl on her hip. "Sit down and I'll hand her to you. But be prepared. She'll do her best to wiggle right out of your arms."

Booker looked around. Both R.J. and Cannon had left. Good. They wouldn't see him make a fool of himself trying to corral a seven-month-old.

Booker took the rocker R.J. had vacated. Brit handed him the baby. Kimmie grabbed a button on his shirt and tried to bite it.

"Is she hungry?"

"No, she's just starting to teethe. She tries to bite everything."

Kimmie drooled on his shirt and then twisted around and put out her arms for Brit to take her back.

"That's your uncle Booker," Brit said in that cooey voice women reserved for talking to babies too young to talk back. "He's come all the way from California to meet you."

Kimmie began to wail and practically threw herself from his arms to get back to Brit.

"I don't think she's into forming family ties," Booker

said. "Maybe I should come back when she starts learning to ride her first bike."

"A big, strong guy like you can't let a baby buffalo him."

"Wanna bet?"

Brit gave in and took Kimmie from his arms. "Aren't you ashamed, young lady, for giving Uncle Booker that kind of welcome?"

Kimmie looked at him from the safe confines of her mother's arms and smiled sheepishly.

"She's just showing me who's boss," Booker said.

"She is a little conniver," Brit agreed, "and she definitely runs this household."

"I can tell. I'm sure R.J. spoils her rotten."

"We all do. But R.J.'s neighbor, Carolina Lambert, says he's like a different man now that he's bonded with so many of his children and grandchildren."

"Tell me about that will of his," Booker said.

"What do you know already?"

"That he had one drawn up when he was first diagnosed with the brain tumor and then had the family reading immediately? Jade indicated that all his children showed up expecting him to be dead."

"That's the way Cannon tells it, too. And if being alive wasn't shock enough, the stipulations for being included in the inheritance were more than a bit bizarre."

"Winner takes all?"

"No, it was fair, more or less. To be included, you had to move onto the Dry Gulch Ranch while R.J. was still living and then you had to stay for one year. Not just live on the ranch but take part in its operation."

"Leif's a defense attorney. Travis is a homicide cop. That doesn't sound like full-time ranch work to me."

"True," Brit admitted. "R.J. bends the rules at will.

What he really wants is a chance to get to know his children. Not that it makes up in any way for his having been a lousy no-show dad for years, but somehow it's working for four of his five sons."

"And is being a full-time wife and mom working for you?"

"For now, but I'll probably go back into law enforcement when Kimmie is older. It's in my blood, the way being a SEAL must be in yours."

"It's my life," he admitted. Love. Marriage. He could see wanting them one day, but that would be years down the road.

Kimmie started to whine and push her chubby little hand into Brit's jaw.

"Time for Kimmie's breakfast," Brit said. "She's not shy about letting me know."

"I can see that."

"Do you want to come in and help feed her?"

"That has all the makings of a catastrophe, but I may give it a try before I leave. Right now I think I'll take a walk."

"Try the worn path out back. It leads to the horse barns. R.J. has some magnificent animals."

Booker needed the walk for more than just exercise. He found the Dalton family a fascinating mix of strangers merging into family.

But for now, Jade was the Dalton who claimed his mind. She was in danger of losing her freedom—if not her life.

"I DON'T KNOW what you did different with those grits, Hadley, but those were the best I've ever eaten."

"Thanks. I have a new Cajun cookbook, and that looked like a good recipe to start with."

"Are there any more of those biscuits?" Booker asked. "I haven't had biscuits like that since I was a kid visiting my grandpa's ranch up in Oklahoma."

"Your wish is my command." Leif's wife, Joni, stepped up with a tea-towel-covered basket of fresh biscuits and set them in front of Booker. "Hot from the oven."

Even R.J. seemed to have a bit more spring in his step this morning. Saturday-morning breakfasts were apparently a fun and calorie-laden event with the Daltons. This morning it was spread on three large picnic tables lined end to end beneath a cluster of oak trees in their full spring glory.

Booker seemed to fit right in, sitting next to R.J. and eating like a starved man. But then, how often did anyone get a breakfast like this? Sausage, bacon, eggs cooked a variety of ways, home fries, grits, biscuits, muffins and an assortment of homemade jams and jellies.

The bounty was wasted on Jade. She forced down a blueberry muffin as she kept waiting for the next bomb to drop. When most had pushed their plates away and moved on to their last few sips of coffee, Brit scooted down to take the chair next to Jade's. "I hope we haven't overwhelmed you with family this morning."

"A little maybe," she admitted. "Is it always like this?"

"It's always noisy and fun when we all get together."

"That must be constantly. You all live so close."

"But we all have our own busy lives. That said, you are the main topic of conversation and concern now," Brit said.

"That should end soon. I'll turn myself in to the police today and then all of you can go back to your own busy lives."

"Not just yet," Brit said. "Leif wants to talk to you

about your next move. He's a brilliant attorney. You should heed his advice."

"I'm willing to listen," Jade said. That was all she'd promise. They all seemed sincere and eager to help. But, in the end, this was her life and she had to take control of it again.

Still, having a brilliant attorney to represent her couldn't hurt.

"I think the front porch is free and quiet for the moment if that works for you," Brit suggested.

"It works."

Minutes later, Leif and Booker joined Jade and Brit on the wide front porch. Booker took the seat next to Jade on the porch swing.

Leif started things off. "First, I should make it clear that I can't serve as your attorney, Jade."

Any optimism she'd felt listening to Brit died with that proclamation. So much for family ties.

"I understand," Jade said, doing her best to hide her disappointment. "I've already heard that you're very busy with your current caseload." One that no doubt paid well.

"I'm neck deep in a very important case, but that wouldn't keep me from taking on yours."

"Is it because it's a case you think you can't win or that you're not convinced of my innocence?"

"Neither. It's a case of protocol and sending the right message. Having a relative defend you can hurt if this goes to a jury trial. Not that I expect it to, but we have to consider all possible investigation outcomes.

"In any case, I've talked to a good friend of mine who practices in the state of New York. John Boros is not only a super guy but he's a brilliant defense attorney. He's won some major cases where the odds were stacked against him. If you're interested, he's agreed to meet with you and hopefully take your case."

"When would that happen?"

"I've made the arrangements for him to fly down tonight if you're interested."

"I'm interested, but I doubt I can afford him."

"It's pro bono, as a favor to me. R.J.'s agreed to cover Boros's expenses."

"Thanks." Jade was awed by the offer, but the simple thanks was all she could manage.

"Then we'll move forward on what we've talked about," Brit said. "I hate to say it, but we need to make sure you've contacted the NYPD before Travis and Faith get back from Washington. There is no way he'll go along with harboring a fugitive at the ranch."

"I agree with Travis," Jade said. "My being here puts you all in the position of breaking the law. I should get a hotel."

"Let's at least wait and hear what John says," Leif urged. "It's not like we're actually harboring you. We're arranging for you to turn yourself in."

"That's a thin line," Jade said. "But I'll stay until I talk to John Boros."

"A smart choice, if I do say so myself," Leif said.

"But for now why don't you and Booker get out and have some fun," Brit suggested. "Take a long walk. Take the ATVs through the ranch's namesake dry gulch. Go for a horseback ride out to Shadow Junction."

"But take a gun," Leif cautioned. "It's warm enough that rattlesnakes will be out again. Water moccasins, too, if you go down to the river."

Horseback riding and shooting snakes with a killer on her tail and the NYPD itching to charge her with murder.

Sure, just get out and have some fun. Only in Texas

and on the Dry Gulch Ranch would you hear advice like that when the odds were stacked so thoroughly against you.

FAITH'S SON, CORNELL, had the horses saddled and waiting outside the horse barn when Booker and Jade arrived on the scene.

Anticipation heightened Booker's excitement as he admired their mounts. He hadn't visited the horse barn this morning as R.J. had suggested, but if these two were representative of the rest of the animals, he wished he had.

Two mares, one chestnut, one black. Both absolutely regal. He'd never ridden anything this magnificent.

"Isn't there a smaller horse you can saddle up for me?" Jade asked. "Perhaps one I don't need help to mount?"

"You're not afraid of old Tornado here, are you?"

"Tornado? As in throws people around like they were toothpicks?" Jade shook her head and backed away. "How about one named Sweet? Or Gentle?"

Cornell laughed. "Just teasing you. Susie Q's big, but she's gentle as they come. R.J. said to put you on her. She'll baby you like you were her own foal."

Jade didn't look as if she was quite a believer yet.

Booker stepped over and gave Susie Q a good nose scratching and then ran a hand along her withers. She stood perfectly still. "Seems calm enough to me. I'll be right beside you and we won't go faster than a steady trot."

"A slow trot," Jade modified. "I'm a city girl. The most dangerous thing I ride is a New York taxi."

Booker took the horse's reins from Cornell. "Then you can survive anything."

"I'll cast my vote on that when we get back."

"But you have ridden a horse before, haven't you?" Cornell asked.

"Not in several years, but I actually got pretty good at it my last trip to summer camp. That was when I was fifteen."

"It hasn't changed that much," Booker assured her.

"Your horse is named Kentucky," Cornell told Booker, "'cause that's where she's from. She's high-spirited, but she's smart and easy to manage. She'll be attentive to every tug on the reins."

"I'm sure Kentucky and I will become fast friends."

Booker helped Jade mount, showing her how to hold the reins in her left hand along with a handful of mane and place the other hand on the horn, standing straight before swinging her right leg into the stirrup.

Once mounted, they trotted along side by side, the horses following a trail through the wooded area behind the house as if they knew exactly where they were going. Within minutes, Jade looked relaxed in the saddle.

He had an idea nothing scared her for long. But she needed to hold on to a healthy fear of Reggie Lassiter, at least enough for her to let Booker hang around. All his instincts screamed that she hadn't seen the last of Reggie yet.

"You must already rue the day I kissed you in the airport," Jade said.

"I'm not sure. I can't remember much about it," he teased. "How about showing me what that was like again?"

"Maybe later, Booker Knox, if you behave yourself. And when it happens, I guarantee you that you will not forget it."

"Then why wait?"

"A second kiss should never be rushed."

Chapter Eight

Brit had been right. Jade had definitely needed to get out of the house. The horseback ride worked wonders at reducing the anxious tension that had become her constant companion.

She owed that more to Booker than to the horse. His confidence and teasing made her feel safe without trivializing the situation. He was growing on her fast.

She had to watch that and not read too much into his protective ways. He was a Navy SEAL. He was used to riding to the rescue. He'd do the same for anyone in trouble.

They dismounted at the horse barn, left their horses in the care of a young ranch hand and walked back to the house together.

She looked out over the fenced pastures that stretched as far as she could see to the east and to a distant stand of pines to the west.

"How many acres does the Dry Gulch cover?" Booker asked.

"I have no idea. I don't even know how many acres would be average for a North Texas ranch."

"Weren't you curious about the size and value when you heard the details of the will?"

"I knew the worth of the estate. R.J. told us it was a little over eight million dollars."

"Not enough for you to even consider living on the ranch for a year?"

"I don't like to be manipulated. And I like the excitement of a big city. I think I'd die of boredom rocking on the front porch and swatting at mosquitoes every night."

"Then it's not all about resentment toward R.J."

"Not all, but it's difficult to feel close to a father who never bothered getting to know you until he found out he was dying."

"He's definitely worried about you now."

Jade let the comment go without offering a response.

When they reached the house, she headed straight for the kitchen to look for a soda. She ran into Brit in the hallway, and the look on Brit's face was a clear sign of trouble.

"Bad news?" Jade asked.

Brit nodded. "We need to talk."

BOOKER AND JADE sat across from Brit at the old kitchen table, which seemed to be the favored spot for dealing with trouble. Not turning herself in to the police today had been his idea. He hoped that wasn't already coming back to burn her.

Jade's hands were wrapped around the glass of diet soda, the condensation dripping from her fingertips. "No sugarcoating," Jade said. "Whatever you have to tell me, I'd rather you just give it to me straight."

That was his girl.

"A fisherman found a body floating under the dock at the Lassiters' fishing camp."

"The one where I was kept hostage?"

"It appears to be the same one. The body had become

entangled in an old fishing trap. The man who found it indicated it had been there for several days."

"Reggie?" Booker asked.

"I don't know. The body was found less than an hour ago and is still listed as unidentified."

"It can't be Reggie," Jade argued. "If it is, I didn't kill him. I swear he was alive when I left there."

Her voice rose as the panic and confusion set in. "But it must be Reggie. Who else would have been there?"

Jade took her hands from the glass and clasped them in front of her.

Booker laid a hand over hers. "It might be an accidental-drowning victim who just happened to get caught under that particular dock."

"The death wasn't accidental," Brit said. "The man was found with a fish-filet knife in his chest."

"Then if it was Reggie, he definitely didn't die at my hands," Jade asserted. "I stabbed him in the back. But if it is Reggie, who would have killed him?"

"Maybe the accomplice who actually stole the necklace," Booker offered. "Or an accomplice who believed Reggie had the necklace and was double-crossing him."

"There's no way of knowing at this point," Brit said. "We can't even verify that Reggie is the victim, yet. He could be the one who did the stabbing."

"If it's Reggie's body, the police will try to pin that murder on me, too," Jade said. "My fingerprints are all over that fishing camp. They might even still be on the knife if it's the same one I stabbed him with."

"They won't find prints on the knife if it's been underwater for days," Booker said.

"I've made a terrible mistake. I should have called the police as soon as I was out of immediate danger. They might have believed me then when the bruises around my wrist were fresh. At that point the police might even have found Reggie alive at the cabin."

"Monday-morning quarterbacking isn't going to get you anywhere," Booker said. "So don't even go there. You were scared. Besides, I'm not convinced that going on the run didn't save your life.

"When was the last time the police had contact with Reggie Lassiter?" Booker asked.

"The night of the murder. He called the precinct about eleven o'clock and claimed he'd gone to Vaquero's penthouse suite to check on why neither he nor Jade had made it to the big event. He found the man dead then."

"That's not true," Jade protested. "He'd killed Quaid hours before that. We'd just drunk the drugged champagne when he came barging in."

"But by eleven he would have had time to remove you from the suite and search for the necklace."

"I still can't figure out how anyone knew that Quaid was going to have the necklace in his suite," Jade said. "I didn't even know until he fastened it around my neck."

Brit's expression grew even more anxious. "Could you identify in a lineup the other two men you said were with him?"

"No. My vision was blurry by then and everyone seemed to be floating."

"But you're sure there were two men?"

"Not absolutely sure. There could have been more."

"Or fewer?"

"Possibly. I was struggling to hold on to consciousness."

"But you're sure you saw Reggie?" Booker asked.

"I heard his voice. It was him. He admitted it was him when he had me locked in that room. He admitted to killing Quaid. And if I'd had the necklace to give him, I'm sure he would have killed me, too."

"Reggie was scheduled to start his vacation leave the morning following the murder. After he called in the murder, his supervisor reportedly told him to go ahead once the crime-scene unit arrived, but to leave a number where they could reach him if they had questions. They also warned him he might have to return to the department on short notice."

"The perfect crime," Jade said. "He had it planned to perfection. He'd have the necklace worth over two hundred million dollars. Quaid and I would be dead and he'd be home free."

"Only now he may be dead and the necklace is still missing," Booker said.

Jade sipped her drink and stared off into space. "Poor Quaid. His career was just taking off. His talent was amazing and he was just beginning to get all the accolades he deserved."

"All for a necklace that so few people saw and no one can find," Brit said.

"So Reggie has disappeared, there's another death and I'm still the prime suspect," Jade said. "Am I missing anything?"

"There's a warrant out for your arrest, and bulletins with your picture on it have been distributed across the country. A New York jeweler has offered ten thousand dollars for information leading to your arrest and conviction."

"Which will bring out all the bounty hunters," Booker said.

Jade pushed back from the table. "It doesn't matter at this point. I just want this over with. There's no use dragging anyone further into my sinkhole. I'm calling the NYPD and telling them I'm ready to turn myself in."

"You can't do that," Booker said.

"I can if one of you will lend me your phone."

"Leif's already left for Dallas," Brit said. "He has a couple of errands to run and then he wants Booker to drive you to his office to meet with John Boros. You need an attorney, and this guy has flown in just to meet with you."

"The least you can do is talk to him," Booker argued.

"Fine," she agreed reluctantly. "But don't hold your breath waiting on a miracle."

"I won't," Booker said. "I'm counting on truth and justice."

"I'm going upstairs for a shower," Jade said. "Call me when it's time to leave for Leif's office."

Booker hated to see Jade like this, but he could understand it. The deck was seemingly stacked against her. But she was a fighter. She'd proved that when she broke free from Reggie. She'd make it through this given time. His job was to keep her alive until she did.

"I hope to God Reggie is dead," Brit said. "That would make one less murderous monster walking the streets."

"But it doesn't make it any safer for Jade," Booker said. "Reggie was not in this alone. If the man who killed Reggie believes there's even a chance that Jade has that necklace, she's still the target of a killer."

"Some days it seems you just can't win," Brit lamented.

"Some days it just takes more to get the job done," Booker challenged.

But it sure would help if something would fall Jade's way.

LEIF'S OFFICE WAS empty when they arrived. Booker let them in with a key Leif had given him. In two short days,

Booker had become a trusted member of the Dalton clan. He fit right in, but then he probably fit in anywhere he went. No pretense with him, or if there was, Jade hadn't spotted it yet.

The office was nothing like what she'd imagined. It was in an old house in downtown Oak Grove. The conversion from house to office space had resulted in a dramatic blend of both.

The waiting room had the warmth of a family room with comfortable furniture in deep browns and greens, a muted patterned rug that reminded her of autumn in Central Park and plantation shutters at a trio of long, narrow windows.

Crown molding and an antique brass chandelier added just the right touch of homey refinement. The flowery scent of the fresh blossoms in a cut-glass vase filled the room.

"There must be big demand for Leif's services if his Dallas clients drive all the way out to Oak Grove to see him."

"I looked him up online," Booker said. "He's handled and won some really big cases both here and in California before he moved to Dallas."

"Who else in my family did you check out?"

"You," he admitted.

"I'd hate to even think what's circulating in the social media about me."

"I'm not into social media, but you have a solid reputation as an event planner."

"I've no doubt seen the last of those. I'm certain I've been fired from my current firm. Not that I'm sweating that right now. I've got far too many other worries to claim my energy."

"If Leif's buddy Boros is half as good as his reputation, you may be celebrating by Monday night."

"Great, as long as no one pops a bottle of champagne. I never want to taste that again."

"We'll have diet soda."

"I can go for that. I suppose you checked out John Boros, too."

"I started with him. Hell of a résumé. Lost his first four cases right out of law school. Hasn't lost one since. Forty-seven years old. Married twice, currently divorced."

"Maybe I should fix him up with my mother. She's searching for husband number six."

"What happened to the first five?"

"Believe me, you don't want to go there."

"Try me."

It finally dawned on Jade that Booker was just making small talk to keep her mind off the upcoming meeting with Boros. It had almost worked.

She began to pace as the hopelessness of her situation hit front and center again. By Monday evening, she would likely be in jail.

Quaid hadn't even had it that good.

Once John Boros arrived, he got right down to business. The introductions were so brusque they bordered on rude. He apparently didn't believe in wasting time on preliminaries.

Nor did he believe in having extraneous people in the room. He relegated both Booker and Leif to the waiting area and he and Jade took Leif's office. Boros took the power seat behind Leif's desk.

And then he bombarded her with questions. She felt as if she were on the witness stand and he was counsel

for the prosecution. She was almost positive he didn't believe a word of her story.

"Are you sure you were already wearing the two-hundred-million-dollar-plus necklace when the champagne was delivered?"

"I'm positive. Quaid had just fastened it around my neck and wanted me to look at myself in the mirror."

"The mirror in his bedroom?"

"No, the mirror was in the living area of the suite."

"Did you make a habit of going to his suite before the showings?"

"No. It was the first time I'd even been inside his suite. He asked me to stop by. I knew he was very excited about the final US showing, so I did. I didn't want to wear the necklace. In fact, I was horrified that he had something so valuable just lying around his hotel suite."

"Where were his other pieces?"

"Already in the showroom, in locked glass cases like you'd find in a jewelry store or a museum with armed security all around."

"And Reggie was head of the security."

"For that night. His brother, Mack, had been there all the other nights to supervise. But that night, he'd put Reggie in charge."

The questions went on and on until she was so weary of them that her head began to pound.

Finally Jade got up from her chair and walked to the window that overlooked a flower garden in a parklike setting that hadn't been visible from the waiting room. "If you're trying to catch me in a lie, it's not going to happen. I'm telling you the truth."

He nodded, rubbed his chin thoughtfully and then started in with the questions again.

"You're sure the room-service guy who Reggie claimed put the drugs in your drink saw you in the necklace."

"I'm sure I had it on. Whether or not he noticed it, I can't say."

"You said there were so many jewels it cascaded into your cleavage. Trust me, he noticed. Would you recognize him if you saw him again?"

"I think so, even though I wasn't paying particular attention to him."

"That's understandable. While you were being awed by Mr. Vaquero's necklace, he was fawning all over you."

"I did not use the word *fawning*."

"A minor detail. But I think I've heard enough."

"Then I shouldn't take up any more of your time."

"Not tonight. Leif is driving me back to Dallas for dinner and then to my room near the airport. I'll be flying back to New York in the morning. I have a lot of work to do before we talk to the NYPD on Monday morning."

"Before *we* talk to the police? Does that mean you're taking my case?"

"Assuming you still want me to."

"Yes." He was formidable. Of course she wanted him on her side.

"Before we leave here I'll need any names or contact numbers you have for Quaid Vaquero's office, home, friends, family or business associates back in Barcelona."

"I only have the numbers to his design studio."

"Then I'll have one of my clerks look into finding more. And you should be aware that the police received a warrant that first day to search your apartment."

"So they could look for the bodies of more of my victims?" she asked sarcastically.

"Purportedly to make sure you weren't there, since

they couldn't locate you and you weren't answering your phone. But you can be sure they searched for the necklace while they were there."

"It's amazing how fast I went from professional career woman doing my job to suspected murderer."

"Quaid's notoriety played a hand in that. Once the media took the little information they had and ran with it, the case became high priority."

"Still, my spotless reputation should have counted for something."

"It will. I'll see to that. I'll expect you to fly to New York tomorrow afternoon. Check in a hotel in the Lower Manhattan area so that you won't get stuck in morning traffic. I'll expect you in my office at eight Monday morning so that we can go over how you need to handle the police interview."

"You mean, handle my arrest, don't you?"

"Not if I can help it. If the investigative team has done their work, they should have at least some evidence that points to Reggie Lassiter as a suspect. He's the one they need to arrest."

"Reggie is dead. I just assumed you knew."

"Reggie is not dead. His brother, Mack, examined the body found beneath their deck, and it is definitely not Reggie. That's not official but it's accurate."

"Who was it?"

"That's undetermined, but the more important question is who killed this man and why. That's where Reggie and the missing necklace come in."

"I'm glad you feel confident about all this, because I don't. But we won't be staying in a hotel that night. We'll be at my apartment."

"I don't recommend it."

"I have to stop by there and pick up some clothes, so we may as well spend the night there."

"Be certain Booker is with you when you go to your apartment. Don't take any risks with your life."

Boros picked up his notes and slid them into his leather briefcase. "I think we've covered enough for tonight."

"You didn't ask me if I have the necklace."

"I don't have to. I can tell when someone's lying. You aren't. Besides, you're not a fool. If you had the necklace, you'd be out of the country by now, not sitting around chatting with me."

He stood and handed her a business card. "Remember, you and Booker in my office at eight o'clock sharp Monday morning."

"You want Booker there, too?"

"I don't expect you to travel anywhere without your bodyguard until Reggie Lassiter is behind bars. A man who's killed twice won't hesitate to kill again."

"Booker is not my bodyguard. He's just a friend."

"You need to take that up with Booker."

She definitely would.

Booker and Jade had dinner that night at what was billed as Oak Grove's finest steak house. It was as bare bones a restaurant as you could get. Round wooden tables with white butcher paper for tablecloths. Regular kitchen chairs. An uneven slate floor.

"If this is tops, what do you think the competition looks like?" Jade said as they stepped inside.

"Steaks still on the hoof."

"Or made of hamburger," she said.

"Whoa, did you just crack a joke, Jade Dalton?"

"I do believe I did."

"I like this John Boros guy already."

"He did boost my confidence a bit."

The hostess dressed in formfitting jeans and a breast-hugging white shirt that tied just below the breasts took them to the table in the back corner that Booker requested.

He ordered a bottle of cabernet, a salad, a baked potato and a large T-bone. Jade ordered a salad and a filet of tenderloin. Once they'd given their order, Jade filled him in on the interview, including the fact that the body found in the river was not Reggie's.

"I'm not surprised," Booker said.

"Is that why you've passed yourself off as my bodyguard?"

"I told you I had your back. I can't very well do that if I'm not around."

"You really don't have to do this, Booker. You only have a short time off before it's back to duty."

He reached across the table and took both her hands in his. "I want to do it, Jade. I want very much to spend my leave with you and to keep you safe."

A wave of unexpected passion whirled through her. It was not the time to be feeling these emotions. Not the place. Yet she'd never been more attracted to any man in her life than she was to Booker at this moment.

Fortunately the steaks were delivered to their table before she lost all control.

The steaks were cooked to perfection and absolutely to die for. For the first time in days, Jade ate a full meal and actually tasted the food.

The rest of the family was in bed by the time they returned to the ranch. Booker walked her to the door of her guest room.

"You know what, Booker Knox?"

"You're tipsy from too much wine."

"Maybe a little, but I think it's time for the second kiss."

Chapter Nine

Booker's good judgment vanished as Jade's arms wrapped around his neck. He captured her lips with his and he was done for. The thrill sent blood rushing to his head, making him dizzy with desire.

He leaned against the door frame and pulled her against him as the kiss deepened. Her lips opened and the taste of her rocked his soul. When his lungs ached from lack of air, he held her even tighter, nibbling her lips and then trailing her neck with kisses.

His body burned with need, his erection pushing hard against the jeans zipper. His thumbs outlined her nipples through the cotton blouse. They pebbled at his touch.

His lips found hers again as he fumbled with the buttons of her blouse until it opened. He tugged the right breast from the bra and found it with his mouth.

Jade reached her hand between his legs and felt the hard length of his arousal. Fighting not to explode, he finally came to his senses.

She was tipsy, vulnerable, her life mired in uncertainty. A kiss was one thing. Good or bad, making love took things to a new level that left no room for going back.

He couldn't risk it, not with her life in his hands.

"You need some rest," he whispered, his voice so

husky with desire he barely recognized it. "I need to cool off."

"But I was right, wasn't I?" she whispered.

She was talking in riddles or he was so far gone he couldn't think straight. "Right about what?"

"Our second kiss would be one you'd never forget."

"I'll let you know when I celebrate my hundredth birthday," he teased. Scary thing was that even if he lived to be a hundred, he knew she was right.

JADE WOKE AT the first light of day. She'd spent a restless night, waking often, lying awake for long periods of time before mental and emotional exhaustion would let sleep claim her again. Her emotions were in a state of riotous flux.

Her feelings about the kiss vacillated between hunger for more and anxiety. She was tantalized by Booker, falling so hard and so fast she couldn't think straight where he was concerned. Had he taken her right there in the hallway, she would have had no inhibitions, held nothing back.

There couldn't be a worse time for her to fall in love, or lust or whatever their relationship was becoming.

The decision had been made and plans were being finalized for her to go to the police and turn herself in. John Boros would walk her through it. He was experienced in working with the NYPD and he believed in her. She had that in her favor.

Reggie Lassiter was still alive and no doubt still wanted her dead. The image of him coming at her, madness gleaming in his eyes, still had the power to fill her with fear.

The house was Sunday-morning quiet. She expected

everyone was still asleep as she threw her legs over the side of the bed and walked to the window.

From the upstairs window, she could see clusters of azalea bushes down the hill from the big house. The watermelon-red blossoms were in full bloom. As she watched, a bluebird flew from a wooden birdhouse mounted on a pole near the flowers.

A deer stepped into view, quickly followed by two spotted fawns.

Jade felt a sudden longing to be out there with the deer, taking in all the scents, sights and sounds of a world so very different from her own.

She dressed hurriedly in a pair of white shorts and a bright blue T-shirt on loan from Brit, slipped into a pair of sneakers borrowed from Hadley and tiptoed out of the bedroom and down the stairs.

She walked into the kitchen on her way to the back door. Movement startled her and she turned to see R.J. fumbling with a coffee filter as he tried to fit it into the coffeemaker.

"Need some help?" she offered.

He turned but stared into space instead of at her.

"Gwen?"

"No, it's me, Jade."

"Where's Gwen?"

He started to shake. The filter slipped from his fingers and fell to the floor. He began to weave as if he was drunk or about to faint.

Jade hurried over and took his arm to steady him before he fell.

"Go get Gwen," he demanded. "I need Gwen."

Jade had no idea who Gwen was, but if she didn't get him into a chair quickly he was going to fall on his face.

"You need to sit down, R.J. Let me help you to your chair and I'll go find Gwen."

"Who are you? What did you do with my coffee?"

She had to do something quick. He was having a stroke or worse. She managed to get him into a chair and was rushing to wake up Booker, when she heard a door open and saw Brit step into the downstairs hallway.

"Is something wrong?"

"It's R.J. I found him in the kitchen trying to make coffee. He's asking for someone named Gwen and he's staring into space as if he's in a trance."

"It's the tumor," Brit said. "There's nothing we can do but watch over him until the lapses lift. Some days are worse than others."

They rushed back to the kitchen together. R.J. was still in the chair where Jade had left him, staring into space.

Brit sat down next to him and took his thin, bony hand in hers. "Good morning, Dad."

Dad. She'd called him Dad, although he wasn't. She and Cannon hadn't even been married all that long, yet the word *dad* had seemed to roll off her tongue effortlessly.

Jade had never called anyone Dad.

"Guess who's here with us?" Brit said, trying to coax R.J. back into reality.

He shook his head, but the vacant stare disappeared. He turned his focus to Brit. "I don't know."

"Your daughter, Jade, is here, Dad. She came all the way from New York to see you."

He rubbed his chin and hugged his arms around his chest. "Jade's here," he said with authority as if he were the one setting Brit straight. "Booker's here, too. I like that boy. He's good for our Jade."

"And she's good for him. It's very early, Dad. Do you want to go back to bed and sleep awhile longer?"

"Now, I want my dadburn coffee. I think the coffee-maker's broke again."

"Not again," she sympathized. "You go relax in your recliner and I'll see if I can get the dadburn thing to work," she said, mimicking his tone and word choice.

He managed a smile.

Jade took one of his arms and Brit took the other and even with his shaky gait they managed to get him to his chair in the spacious family room. He leaned back but didn't relax. He fidgeted with his shirt collar and the baggy skin at his neck.

Brit handed him a couple of ranching magazines from the coffee table. "Do you mind sitting with him while I get the coffee started?"

"I can make the coffee," Jade suggested. "It will only take me a minute to get it started and then you can go back to bed and grab a little more sleep."

"I'm wide-awake now," Brit said. "Besides, I enjoy a little time to myself in the morning while Kimmie's still sleeping. Once she's up, the day starts full blast. Days are never dull around the Dry Gulch."

Jade couldn't imagine that would be true, not after the fast pace of living in New York. But to each his own.

"Ask R.J. about his horses," Brit said. "Or his grand-children. He can brag about both topics for hours."

"He was asking for someone named Gwen."

"He frequently does when he slips into a state of confusion."

"Who is she?"

"No one knows."

"Could it be one of his wives?"

"No. We checked that out. But apparently there have

been lots of women in his life. I suppose it could be any one of them. Whoever she is, she definitely made a lasting impression on him or at least on his subconscious."

Definitely a lot of women in his life, Jade thought as Brit walked back to the kitchen. Six children by five different wives and he and Jade's mother had never married. Doubly odd since her mother had a tendency to marry every man who showed her a good time.

R.J. thumbed through one of the magazines. Jade decided to forgo Brit's suggested topics and hit on one of her own. "Do you remember Kiki?"

He closed the magazine and looked Jade in the eye. "If you're talking about your mother, damn straight I remember her. Hasn't been that long ago she was living here on the Dry Gulch."

He sounded like himself again, all traces of his earlier confusion vanished.

"It's been twenty-two years."

"Time flies. You look a lot like her, you know?"

"That's what everyone says. Mother complains that I inherited your stubbornness, though."

"If you had to get something from me, that's one of the better traits you could inherit."

"So I've heard."

"Your mother was younger than you when she came to live on the ranch."

"She was twenty when I was born." And R.J. had been in his late fifties. "How did my mother end up on the Dry Gulch Ranch?"

"Didn't she tell you that?"

"No." Not even when Jade had asked.

"She got in a fight with her daddy one night and just moved out on her own. Old Ted Seager, meaner than a skillet full of rattlesnakes, that one. Don't know how your grandma ever put up with him."

Grandparents whom Jade had never met and never would now. They had both died years ago. "So my mother moved out of his house and into yours?"

"Not right away. I don't want to talk bad about your mom, but I guess you're old enough to know the truth."

The truth according to R.J.

"I'm sure she's outgrown her wildcat ways," R.J. said, "but back then she was dead set on doing as she pleased, in large part to get back at her pappy."

"What did she do?"

"Got in with the wrong crowd. Was about to go to jail for shoplifting. I offered her a place to stay if they'd put her on probation. Judge had a heart and agreed to give her a delayed sentence as long as she stayed out of trouble."

And then she'd moved in with R.J. and become pregnant. Jade could see that happening. Couldn't even entirely blame R.J. for that. When her mother wanted something, she went after it. Pity the poor man who tried to resist.

When she was pregnant with Jade, she admittedly decided she wanted a career in Hollywood. She'd found a guy—husband number one—who'd promised her that and the moon, and she was off to her next adventure.

But with all her faults, her mother had still been there for Jade. R.J. had never been there, not until he'd found out he was dying. Not until his conscience needed soothing on his way to eternity.

Brit returned with a tray carrying mugs of hot coffee and slices of warm banana bread.

Jade took a coffee and sipped. "That is great. Glad the dadburn coffeemaker is working," she teased.

R.J. grinned. "I should get a new one."

"I hate to leave such good company, but I have a lot on my mind this morning," Jade said. "Would you mind if I take my coffee and go for a walk?"

"I think a walk is an excellent idea," Brit agreed. "When worried, I usually go for a horseback ride. There's just something about brisk morning air and wide-open spaces that helps me put things into perspective. If you'd like, maybe later we can take a couple of the horses who need exercising for a ride."

"I'd like that."

With all Jade had to worry about, this time it was R.J. who preyed on her mind as she stepped out the back door and into a world of sunshine and spring splendor.

"Dad."

She tried saying the word out loud to see how it felt on her tongue. It simply wouldn't work.

STILL REVERBERATING FROM the kiss that he'd let go too far, Booker had spent a good part of the night at his laptop. Another man was dead, most likely killed at the hands of Reggie Lassiter, who was determined to get his hands on the missing necklace.

One fact was certain. The necklace hadn't walked off on its own. Someone had to have it or at least know where it was.

Booker also searched every mention and article he could find regarding Quaid Vaquero. A young Vaquero had started designing jewelry fifteen years ago in a small village on the Bay of Biscay. His wife had died ten years ago.

One year later, the young wife of a wealthy Spanish jewelry-store owner discovered Quaid's genius. She hired him to create some pieces for one of their very special customers. Quaid did and that was the beginning of his rise to fame.

With the fame came money and women, a parade of supermodels and starlets. No doubt he'd been seducing Jade the night he was killed.

Who could blame him? Gorgeous, smart, spunky as hell, Jade Dalton was impossible to resist.

Could jealousy have played a part in his murder? One of Quaid's lovers? One of Jade's? But how would the necklace and Reggie Lassiter fit into that scenario?

Booker kept reading. Quaid had no family but was apparently fond of his young, female assistant, Zoe Aranda. Her older brother, Javier, had been his best friend growing up.

Quaid had taken Zoe to Barcelona with him and built her a villa and a design studio overlooking the water less than a mile from his frequently photographed mansion.

Booker tried to picture a scenario where either Zoe or Javier fit into the murder and theft, but it was difficult to imagine either of them plotting such an elaborate scheme from halfway across the world.

Difficult but not impossible. He wondered if the NYPD were investigating them or if they were banking all their expectations of guilt on Jade. If so, it would make it doubly hard on her tomorrow.

He should be doing more to help her get this all straightened out. Protecting her was important, but knowing exactly what Reggie was up to and where he was would make him feel a whole lot better.

He turned off the computer and pulled on a black sport shirt. He'd heard Jade go downstairs earlier. He'd resisted the temptation to join her. Last night had been a mistake.

Now a brush of their shoulders, a smile across the table, a horseback ride would ignite the passion all over again. The only thing he needed to be obsessed with was keeping her safe, especially now that they were heading back to Reggie's turf.

He went to the bathroom, raked his hair back in place and went down to join the Daltons. And Jade.

And with that thought, the hunger for her revved up again.

REGGIE LASSITER SWALLOWED the last of the stale bagel he'd picked up at the convenience store/service station a block or two down from his lousy hotel. He reached for the lukewarm coffee to wash it down.

He'd always wanted to come to Atlanta, but not like this, not holed up in some roach-infested motel under an assumed name. But this was the best place not to be noticed.

He'd tracked Jade this far before the trail had turned cold. He'd pick it up again soon and this time he'd get the necklace or leave her dead.

He'd been too soft on her at the fishing cabin. When he found her this time, he wouldn't be. If it took torture to make her cough up the necklace, then torture it would be. She had it coming.

His new untraceable cell phone rang. It had to be Mack. He was the only who had the number, and that was just so Mack could keep him up-to-date on how this was being played out in the New York media.

"Hello, Mack," he answered. "What's up?"

"Are you watching the news?"

"Not at the moment."

"Turn it on CNN."

"Give me a minute." He flicked on the TV and surfed until he landed on the channel.

Breaking news. He listened, stunned.

"Jade Dalton's attorney confirms that she will be turning herself in to the New York City Police Department tomorrow sometime before noon. He insists that she's innocent and that she has information that may…"

"If she didn't kill Vaquero, who do you think did it?" Mack asked.

"She killed him."

"Then I hope they have enough solid evidence to keep her in jail. Having Quaid get murdered on our watch is bad for business. I've had three cancellations already."

"Things will calm down soon." At least they would for Reggie. Once he got his hands on that necklace, he was long gone.

"How's your vacation going?" Mack asked.

"Super. Soaking up the sun. Gotta run now. I'm missing the beach action."

Reggie broke the connection. He wasn't about to get into some long-winded conversation about his nonexistent vacation.

He picked up the cardboard coffee cup and threw it across the room. Brown liquid splattered the bed and the walls.

That auburn-haired, two-bit slut was going to tell the cops everything except that she had the necklace. Her testimony would send him up the river and she'd come out looking like a victim.

When things died down, she'd just buy a ticket to paradise, dump the necklace on the black market and live the life that was supposed to have been his.

He wouldn't let her away with it. He'd kill her first.

He tossed his clothes into his duffel and then threw

the duffel into the trunk of his car. If he was going to kill Jade, the sooner the better.

Before she talked to the police.

Before they sent him away for life.

Chapter Ten

Jade walked until hunger pains were rattling around in her stomach. They grew worse as she neared the back of the house and scents of bacon, cinnamon and coffee wafted on the morning breeze.

Jade took the back steps. Surprisingly, the kitchen did not have the swarm of people who had congregated for breakfast the day before. Only R.J. with his morning newspaper and—

She stopped and stared as her mind took in the rest of the scene. Booker was pushed back from the table holding a baby bottle and coaxing Kimmie to take the nipple in her mouth.

"How was the walk?" Brit asked as she set a plate full of warm muffins on the table.

"It was great. Sorry I was gone so long. I should have helped with breakfast."

"No problem," Cannon said. "Sunday's my morning at the cooktop. Pancakes and bacon coming up."

"It smells delicious." It did, but Jade's eyes were still on Booker.

"Don't look so shocked," Booker said. "I am not without skills when it comes to small animals, goldfish and wiggling babies."

"Who'd have guessed?"

"Not Kimmie," Booker said. "She's just teasing me. Takes two sips and then stops to play."

Kimmie kicked playfully and caught a toe with her stubby fingers.

"She likes you better than she did yesterday," Brit said.

"It's my subtle charms. I grow on women."

Jade could vouch for that. "She'll have Uncle Booker wrapped around her fingers in no time."

"I'm not that easy." He flashed her a smile that sent a shiver of awareness zinging along every nerve ending.

"You were up early this morning," Booker said.

"I couldn't sleep. I tried not to wake you, but that one groaning stair step must have given me away."

"I was awake," he said. "Couldn't sleep, either, so I was doing some research on my laptop."

"Did you learn anything useful?"

"What do you know about Zoe Aranda?" he asked.

"She was Quaid's assistant back in Barcelona."

"Did she come to New York with him?"

"No, but he mentioned her several times. I think she's the only one he trusted to work on his designs. I'm sure she's heartbroken over his death."

"From the pictures online, he probably left a lot of broken hearts among the jet-set hotties."

"Possibly," Jade said. "I do know he was very thoughtful and couldn't have been nicer to work with."

"My guess is you were already added to his yacht guest list."

She could almost swear there was a touch of jealousy behind that statement. It shouldn't, she knew, but there was no denying that the possibility pleased her.

"Regardless of what Mr. Vaquero did in his personal life, it's sad that the world lost such a talent to a pointless murder," Brit said.

"It's sad when anyone gets murdered. But c'mon," Cannon said. "Over two-hundred-million-plus dollars for a piece of jewelry. Anyone who'd pay that has to be crazy no matter how rich he is."

"Guess that means you didn't have plans to buy me a Vaquero original for Christmas."

"I was thinking something more in the line of a new bull."

Brit popped him on the butt with the tea towel she was holding. He grabbed her and pulled her into his arms for a kiss.

Jade had no idea how they made married with a baby look not only easy but fun. She went to the sink, washed her hands and finished setting the table while Brit poured coffee and Cannon forked the last of the bacon from the skillet to a serving plate.

R.J. folded his newspaper and shoved it under his chair. "I don't know what this world's coming to. Back when I was learning to drive, you didn't need laws to keep people from texting and driving."

"Back when you were a boy, there were no cars," Cannon teased.

"I had a car. Old Dodge. Tires went flat every time I drove it into town. Didn't need to text. Had a party line. Everybody in town knew what we were up to."

Brit retrieved a few jars of assorted jams from the fridge and set them in the middle of the kitchen table. "Fill your plates. Pancakes are better when they're hot."

R.J. reached across the table and helped himself to a pancake. "Don't have to tell me twice. My backbone's bumping my stomach."

Jade walked over to Booker. "Why don't you let me hold Kimmie while you eat?"

"Better yet, I'll put her in her jump chair," Brit suggested. "If she was interested in that bottle, she'd be sucking, not playing."

"I'll hold her awhile longer," Booker said. "I can always heat my pancake in the microwave for a few seconds, but I have to bond with Kimmie while she'll tolerate me."

This was a side of the tough, sexy SEAL Jade had never expected to see. It touched her but made her uncomfortable at the same time.

He fit in this family as if he were the one who'd been born into it. She was the outsider. What did that say about her?

"What do the rest of the Dry Gulch inhabitants do on Sunday morning?" Jade asked.

"All depends on the weather, who's home and who's working." R.J. drowned his pancake in hot maple syrup he poured from a small pottery pitcher. "Not sure where Leif's daughter, Effie, is this morning, but she'll probably be popping in any second."

"She spent the night with her BFF last night," Brit said. "No doubt they're riding this morning. I've never seen anyone so fond of horses and riding."

"The men cook on Sunday evening," Cannon said. "Usually we just throw some steaks on the grill, drink a few beers and catch up on what's going on with the others while we tend the meat."

"Or watch baseball," Brit said. "The Texas Rangers dictate the spring weekend schedule."

Way too much togetherness for Jade. She saw her mother most Christmases or Thanksgivings. Never both. That usually resulted in enough advice to last a year.

"R.J. is the social center of the family," Brit said. "He has family and neighbors dropping by all the time."

"Sniffing around hoping to get a piece of your chocolate cake," R.J. teased. "I'm just the excuse they use."

They finished breakfast, and Jade and Booker took over the cleanup chores. Working side by side with no one else around to see or hear them was not the best of decisions.

The sexual tension swelled by the second, growing so thick she had to move away from him to calm her pulse rate.

That might have worked if Booker hadn't stepped up behind her, put his arms around her waist and pulled her close. Resistance became impossible.

She turned and slipped her arms around his neck, her fingers tangling in the thick locks of his hair. When his lips touched hers, she melted into the kiss with pure abandonment.

"We shouldn't," he whispered.

"I know."

But then he took her hand and tugged her toward the stairs and she knew that they would.

Chapter Eleven

Ever since the first kiss in the Dallas airport, they'd been moving toward this moment. Jade had fought grief, shock, fear, anxiety and everything else life had thrown at her, but she could no longer fight her need of Booker.

She fell into his arms at the door to her room, her hunger for him tearing down any semblance of common sense or control. Booker lifted her as if she were weightless and carried her to the bed. With one hand, he threw back the pale blue quilt before laying her atop the crisp sheets.

Passion at a fever pitch, Jade pulled him onto the bed beside her and rolled into his arms. She was dizzy with desire and this time when he kissed her, she knew that would never be enough.

Booker nibbled her earlobe. "I've tried not to want you," he whispered. "The harder I try the crazier I become. I don't—"

She stopped his words with two fingers to his lips. "Please don't try to explain this away, Booker. Don't explain me."

"There's no explaining you, Jade Dalton, or the way you make me feel. I'm nuts about the look of you, the feel of you, the taste of you."

He punctuated each phrase with kisses while his right

hand massaged her inner thighs. His touch was slow, tantalizing and deliciously provocative. Anticipation swelled until it was practically torment.

Jade unzipped her shorts and wiggled out of them. Booker helped her along, his fingers catching the edge of her panties, tugging them off and tossing them across the room.

He bent over her, his hands caressing her breasts while he trailed kisses down her abdomen, pausing only a heart-stopping second on her most intimate area before his lips slid to the smooth flesh of her thighs.

His fingers moved back to her shirt, pushing up the knit fabric and then reaching behind her to unclasp her bra. When her breasts fell free, he moaned softly and then took the nipples in his mouth one by one. His hands caressed the soft mounds of flesh while he sucked and nibbled.

He trailed his right hand back down her abdomen, this time stopping to delve into her most intimate area. She felt the heated slickness and her body arched toward Booker's. She had to have him, completely, nothing held back.

"I want all of you, Booker," she whispered. "I want to feel you thrusting inside me."

"Are you sure?"

"More sure than I've ever been of anything in my life."

Jade tugged the shirt over her head and slipped her arms from the bra straps, tossing both items to the floor. In seconds, Booker had shed his clothes, as well.

Her pulse pounded at the sight of him. Naked. Bronzed. Muscular thighs. Six-pack abs. A sprinkling of dark, curly hair on his chest. His desire for her hard and pulsing.

He came back to bed, slipped on protection and straddled her. She reached for his erection and guided it inside her. And then nothing existed for her but the thrill coursing through her body.

They skyrocketed to the crest together. When it was over, he rolled off her and pulled her into the curve of his arms. She cuddled against him, passion-spent, reeling from emotions she didn't fully understand and didn't want to examine.

Words of love rolled around on her tongue, but she held them inside. It was no time for expectations or anything that whispered of the future. Tomorrow she could be locked behind bars. It could be the end of life as she knew it.

But this moment would be forever embedded in her soul.

It WAS SEVEN O'CLOCK on Sunday evening and Jade was back in New York City. She and Booker were in the backseat of a taxi, only a few blocks from her tiny apartment in Greenwich Village. Booker, like the typical tourist, was chatting with the driver during the intervals when said driver was not honking his horn and complaining about weekend drivers.

Even the constant honking didn't bother Jade this evening. Nothing about her situation with the police or being a target of a killer had changed, but her spirits were higher than they had been since waking up as Reggie's prisoner.

Booker got all the credit for the improvement in her. Making love with him that afternoon had left her warm and glowing and feeling *almost* like her usual confident self.

"I know you said you've been to New York before, but have you spent much time in the village?" she asked.

"Some. I have a SEAL buddy whose sister lives here. He invited me to come spend a couple of weeks on my last leave."

"What did you think?"

"That I was being set up and that if I didn't get out of there fast, his sister was going to be booking a church."

"Did you like her?"

"Yeah. I liked her, in small doses. That's all I could take of her endless name-dropping and tales of who'd flirted with her and how."

"Where did she work?"

"At NBC, as a stenographer who harbored unwarranted feelings of grandeur."

"Oh, one of those. The city's full of them."

"So I've heard. Her brother's great, though. Nobody I'd rather have with me on a dangerous mission."

"You can let us out at the next corner," Jade said, addressing their driver. She started to reach for her wallet and then remembered she was down to about three one-dollar bills.

"I'll get it," Booker said, pulling out his billfold.

"Good. I'm flat busted."

He leaned over and whispered in her ear, "Temporarily without funds, but definitely not flat-busted."

Her cheeks burned, but she didn't mind his sexual teasing. It was a good sign that he, like her, was still under the spell of their afternoon delight. Much better than wallowing in depression.

"Two houses down on the left," Jade said once they exited the taxi. "Bear in mind, I've just started to acquire furniture to suit my taste. The rest is the junk-shop chic I had to furnish with originally."

"Junkyard chic would be a step up for me. When

I'm on a mission, a bed might be hard or impossible to come by."

Jail would likely be a step up for Booker on those nights. Yet here he was, spending the little time he had off jumping right back into a dangerous situation to keep her safe.

"There's still time to escape the role of protector," she reminded him as they approached her apartment. "A short taxi ride can take you back to the Theater District, not that it's very lively on Sunday evenings."

"And miss seeing your city flat? Not a chance."

She stopped in front of a store filled with African-artifact imitations. "Then take a look around. This is it."

"You live in a shop?"

"Above it. The owners live on the second floor. I have the third, but I do have a private entrance."

"Where?"

"In the back. Follow me."

She stopped at the foot of the very steep steps.

"No wonder you have great legs," Booker said.

"Thank you."

She started up. He didn't follow, but instead stood on the first step scanning the area.

"You can't find the steps daunting. I've heard of the feats you special ops guys endure in training."

"Is this your only exit?"

So that was it. He didn't keep bringing up the fact that coming back to New York had put her in jeopardy, but he was constantly aware. "There are a set of steps inside the house I could use if there was an emergency."

He nodded. She climbed to the first narrow landing. He followed, still studying the area.

"Exactly what are you looking for?"

"I'm sure the police have been staking out your apartment and still are. I'm just trying to figure out where they're watching from."

Her nerves jumped the tracks again. "Why didn't you say something sooner? We shouldn't have come here." She looked around, expecting officers with guns drawn to come rushing at them any second.

"It doesn't really matter now. They're not going to bust in and arrest you tonight after Boros has made plans for you to turn yourself in."

"They have a warrant for my arrest. Why should they wait until I turn myself in?"

"So you'll be more cooperative and it will give the appearance that they're only after the facts, not to pin a murder on you."

"How do you know so much about how the police work?"

"I had a beer with Leif while you were getting ready for the flight. He is a very astute attorney."

She was no longer at the Dry Gulch Ranch, but it still had a hold on her. It was as if going there had sucked her into a family vacuum from which there was no escape.

Not a prisoner as she'd been with Reggie. Not secured by metal handcuffs, but by invisible ties that were just as strong. She climbed the last flight and waited.

Evidently satisfied with what he saw, Booker bolted up the stairs as if they were flat as an airport tarmac. She retrieved the key from her pocket and inserted it into the lock.

She was home and whether the police were watching or not, the familiarity felt good. Tonight she'd sleep in her own bed, shower in her bathroom. Wear her own clothes—sexy nighties or cloud-soft T-shirts that rode high on her thighs.

When she dressed in the morning, it would be in a

designer suit and matching shoes that accentuated her long legs. An outfit *not* suitable for riding horses.

She opened the door, stepped inside and into a new hell. Her spirits crumbled. Would the nightmare never stop?

Chapter Twelve

Jade stared at the chaos, unable to get her mind around the destruction. It was as if a tornado had torn through the house or a bomb had gone off.

The sofa pillows had been slashed and tossed onto the floor. Lamps were broken. Picture frames smashed. Furniture overturned. Worse, the walls had been spray-painted with black paint.

"I can understand the police watching the apartment and even searching it. But why destroy everything I'd worked and saved so hard to buy?"

"This is not the work of the police, Jade."

"I don't see how anyone else would have had the opportunity to do it. The police had a warrant to search the premises and you said yourself that they've undoubtedly had the apartment staked out."

"Obviously, someone fell asleep on the job."

"Or didn't know about the inside entrance. Do you think Reggie did this?"

"Him or an accomplice, or possibly some crackpot vigilante who felt the need to get back at you for Quaid's murder."

"Murder. Hate. A demolition derby in my apartment. Whatever happened to innocent until proven guilty?"

She squeezed her eyes shut, determined not to let the bitter tears escape.

Booker pulled her shaking body into his arms. "Let's get out of here. We can get a hotel and deal with this after tomorrow."

"You mean wait because if I'm in jail it won't matter if my place is a wreck or not."

"I didn't say that. I just don't see the point of facing this right now."

"I want to see it all, Booker. I want it in my mind when I talk to the police tomorrow. I want them to know what I've been through because of their groundless accusations."

"Then let's get it over with." He took her hand and walked with her into the small kitchen.

The damage was less there. No black paint coating the counters, floors or walls. All the drawers were ajar, however, some yanked from the cabinets with their contents dumped onto the floor.

"Hopefully they grew bored with the..." She sputtered, trying to think of a word horrendous enough to describe the acts of vandalism. She couldn't, so she let the sentence go unfinished.

"I know it's your home and that you feel violated, but they're just things," Booker reminded her. "You got away from Reggie with your life, unlike Quaid Vaquero or the man beneath the dock."

"I know. You're right, of course." Booker was a SEAL. Danger was a staple of his existence, toughness in the line of duty a job requirement. She was not that tough.

Still, she girded about her what strength she had left and strode into the bedroom. It made the living room look like kids' play.

White feathers from what had been her pillows covered the floor like flakes of snow. Her mattress had been carved into shreds. Her sleepwear and unmentionables had been strewn around the room like confetti.

A pair of red lacy panties dangled from the chandelier. A leopard-skin-patterned bra draped a picture frame. A black negligee rested atop a mountain of white feathers.

"Son of a bitch," Booker said. "This is definitely more perversion and revenge than searching for a necklace."

Crushed and bewildered, Jade hung on to a bedpost as the room began to spin. Everything she had was gone. Not only *things* as Booker had said, but her reputation, likely her career, possibly even her freedom.

She ached to lash out at someone, but there was no one to take the brunt of her frustration and anguish.

"You're dealing with too much to tackle this tonight," Booker said. "Let's get through tomorrow and then we'll hire someone to clean up this mess."

"I need to get some clothes before we go, a nice suit to wear tomorrow, a pair of dressier shoes, something to make me feel like myself."

Feeling steadier, she let go of the bedpost and stepped into her walk-in closet. One look and she exploded.

"Ruined," she said, spitting the word out like poison on her tongue. "He spray-painted every piece of my clothing."

Her angst dissolved like ice in a microwave. Fury took its place. She picked up one of her five-pound weights and hurled it at the closet wall, knocking a fist-sized hole in the drywall.

"Reggie Lassiter has to be the one responsible for this. It's the kind of twisted, deranged stunt he'd pull to get back at me or maybe to frighten me into not telling the police the truth about him.

"It won't work. I will help send that murderous bastard

to prison if it's the last thing I do. Call John Boros. Tell him what we found here and that I can't wait for tomorrow."

She stamped past Booker on the way to the door. "I'm ready to go. There's nothing left here that I want."

Booker bent over and rescued her answering machine from a pile of jeans. "We should check your messages first. They could be important."

"You check them," she said. "It's probably hacks or bounty hunters trying to find me and collect the reward."

She stood at the door and waited for him, listening in spite of her claim of disinterest.

There were three calls from her boss begging Jade to please return her phone calls. Not a lot of need for that, since she was probably calling to tell her she was fired. There were at least a half dozen calls from Detective Winston Fielding telling her that it was urgent that he talk to her as a person of interest in the murder of Quaid Vaquero.

Booker quickly skipped past them to the next message.

"Jade, this is Jake Dalton, R.J.'s oldest son. We don't really know each other, but I'd like to offer my help if you need it, presuming your innocence. Call me." He gave two numbers where he could be reached.

"I didn't expect to hear from him," Jade said.

Booker scribbled down his numbers. "Always nice to have offers of support at a time like this."

"I think we're sufficiently saturated with Daltons."

"One last message," Booker said, ignoring her comment.

"Jade. My name is Zoe Aranda. I work for Quaid in Barcelona."

Her voice was so shaky and her accent so pronounced

that Jade had difficulty understanding her. "Hit Replay," she requested after the message cut off. Booker complied.

"I'm in New York to pick up Quaid's body and take it home. Please call me. Very urgent. Must talk."

She left a phone number.

"You can use my phone," Booker said, obviously urging Jade to make the call.

"No use not to use my home phone now," Jade said. "If someone comes here looking for me, I'll be gone."

"Your phone is probably tapped by the police. Zoe may not want them to hear what she has to tell you."

Booker punched in the number Zoe had left and put the phone on speaker so that he could listen in.

No one answered. Jade left a message that she was available if Zoe wanted to call her back. "She may already have gone back to Spain," Jade said. "If not, she's probably heard enough about my being a suspect that she no longer wants to talk to me."

"If the clock on your answering device is set correctly, that call was made today."

"Then hopefully she'll call back."

Jade took one last look around, swallowed hard and walked to the door. "What's your pleasure?" she asked. "A big-money hotel that we'll need to take a taxi to or a neat little boutique hotel about three blocks from here? Either way, I'm paying now that I can use the ATM again."

"Ah, big spender, but I've got this one. You'll need your money for a new wardrobe. Let's go with the hotel we can walk to. Strolling hand in hand in the Big Apple will be a new experience for me."

"Prepare to be underwhelmed."

"No danger of that with you around, Jade Dalton."

They set off, her anger so all-consuming that they'd walked two blocks before she noticed how attentive

Booker was to every detail. His gaze constantly scanned the area.

Either he feared that Reggie or whoever had demolished her apartment might jump from behind a parked car or cluster of pedestrians at any turn or he thought a vigilante-type stranger might recognize her from media photographs and start trouble.

His tenseness made her even angrier. She'd done nothing wrong. She shouldn't have to live in fear. She shouldn't need protecting. He shouldn't have to spend his leave like this.

"Does this hotel have room service?" Booker asked.

"Thankfully, no. Room service is where all this started. Are you hungry?"

"Starved. That sandwich at the Dallas airport wore off over Kansas."

"There's a popular piano bar on the first floor of the hotel. They serve pub food."

"That'll work."

It was a relief when they reached the hotel. "A king or two doubles?" the tall, stately woman at the desk asked.

Booker exchanged a questioning glance with Jade.

"King."

She was up against a killer, but she wasn't about to lie down and play dead yet. If nothing else, her newfound anger had her fired up to take her life back. And that included enjoying every second of being with the hottest, hunkiest, genuine hero she'd ever met.

She'd take him over a diamond-and-emerald necklace any day of the week.

THE PIANO BAR was crowded and noisy. No way was Booker going to risk taking Jade in there. He motioned a waiter to the door, flashed a big bill and found the waiter extremely accommodating.

In under five minutes the waiter returned with a couple of to-go boxes and a small white paper bag. Dinner for their room without resorting to room service.

They took the elevator to the third floor. The room was perfect. Cozy and with a huge bed piled with pillows and a snowy white coverlet. Two inviting white robes were waiting in the closet next to the spacious bathroom.

A perfect lovers' getaway. Too bad that wasn't why they were here.

Booker had expected Jade to feel defeated and down after seeing her wrecked apartment. Instead she was enthused with an anger that had her ready to take on the entire NYPD and Reggie Lassiter, as well.

Booker was just as furious, but even more worried. Destruction that extreme had to have been fueled by a deranged mind set on vengeance.

Booker could not let that person get anywhere near Jade. But this was not a SEAL mission he was leading. He had no official authority and he could be up against the entire NYPD.

"I think I'll grab a shower," Jade said. "The stench of my apartment is probably infused in my skin."

"Good idea. Soap, shampoo and lots of hot water should work miracles."

She kicked out of her shoes, shed the jeans she'd borrowed from Brit and pulled off her top before leaving the bedroom. How in the hell was he supposed to concentrate on solutions with his libido constantly springing into action?

His ringing phone took care of that. He recognized the number at once as belonging to Zoe Aranda. He rushed to the bathroom and handed it to Jade just as she was stepping into the shower. He mouthed Zoe, turned the phone on speaker and handed Jade the phone.

She stepped from beneath the spray. "Hello."

"I'm Zoe, Quaid's friend."

"Yes, I know. He mentioned you often."

"In what way?"

"He said he couldn't have accomplished half of what he did without your help. I know you're grieving for him. I'm so sorry for your loss."

"We need to talk about Quaid's death," Zoe said.

"I know what you're hearing on the news, but I didn't have anything to do the murder or stealing the necklace," Jade said. "It may take me a while to prove my innocence, but I can assure you I did nothing wrong."

"I believe you, but we still need to talk and I can't say what I need to over the phone."

"It's late tonight, but perhaps we could meet somewhere tomorrow afternoon."

"Yes, that would be—"

Background noises drowned her soft voice.

"I couldn't hear you, Zoe."

"I have to go." Her voice was a whisper. The voices in the background grew louder.

"First tell me where to meet you," Jade urged.

Zoe didn't respond. The connection had already been broken.

She handed Booker the phone. He called Zoe back. The call went straight to her recorded message. "She's turned off the phone," he said.

"Because someone walked in on her. I think she was afraid to say more."

"Perhaps whoever she's staying with has warned her not to call you."

"She sounded frightened. She said she knows I didn't kill Quaid. That could be because she knows who did."

"Not likely, but if she has something important to tell you, she'll call back."

"Yes, but I may be in jail by then."

"We'll deal with that problem when we come to it." He was a long way from being resigned to Jade's going to jail. She wasn't guilty, so they couldn't possibly have anything but circumstantial evidence against her.

And she was coming in on her own. That had to count for something.

He left Jade to her shower while he unpacked their food. A bottle of red wine, two deli sandwiches and two slices of apple pie.

They'd have a picnic in bed and hopefully escape reality again at least for an hour or two. She'd be fresh from the shower, clad only in the robe with a tie belt he could loosen in a second. He'd be...

Hell, what was he waiting for? Nothing provided an escape from reality like a shower for two.

BOOKER WAS EXTREMELY impressed with John Boros's knowledge of the law concerning a suspect's rights, but he did not share the attorney's optimism as they finished up their early strategy session. Booker wasn't sure what he'd expected from the attorney, but nothing he'd shared with them this morning backed up his claim that Jade was unlikely to be arrested.

The frightening possibility that she could be thrown into a jail cell before the day was over ground in Booker's gut like shattered glass. This was all miles out of his area of expertise, but the creed "failure is not an option" still held true.

His first priority was keeping Jade safe, but he'd feel a

hell of a lot better about his ability to do that if she were with him instead of behind bars, especially when a dirty cop wanted her dead.

John Boros picked up the phone on his desk and requested his car be delivered to the front of his office. His office was actually most of the fifth floor of a ten-story building less than a half mile from Ground Zero.

"I love this old building with all its character and quaint charm," Boros said as shoved files into a leather briefcase, "but parking is a real pain."

"Where do you park?" Booker asked.

"There's contract parking in the next block. It has a valet service during the day, but work past six as most of us do on a regular basis and you're on your own."

"Not too bad a walk," Booker said. "Beats hiking up a mountain carrying a weapon and hauling a forty-pound pack on your back."

"You're right. I'll make an effort to stop complaining—until its ten degrees, sleet is slapping me in the face and the wind is howling around the corner of the buildings."

Boros stood and pulled on the coat to his stylish navy blue suit. "Remember, Jade. Stick to the truth. Winston Fielding is a bulldog of a homicide detective, but he has great instincts for detecting guilt and innocence. That's another reason I didn't hesitate to take your case."

"Then you've worked with Fielding before," Booker said.

"Several times."

Hopefully that would work to Jade's advantage. They left through the lobby. A black sedan was double-parked in front of the building.

Ever cautious, Booker took in their surroundings with an eye for trouble.

Two men in suits were walking together on the opposite side of the street, to-go coffees in hand. A FedEx truck was double-parked in front of a building two doors down. An elderly gentleman with a cane was standing at the corner waiting for the light to change.

Nothing struck Booker as dangerous or unusual. Not that he had expected it to, but Jade's wrecked apartment last night had been an excellent reminder of the kind of lunatic they were dealing with.

The young valet got out, leaving the door open for Boros, then walked around the front of the car to open the passenger-side door for Jade. Booker followed a step behind them.

The breeze caught Jade's soft auburn curls and she quickly covered her hair with both hands to keep it from blowing into her face. Tension pulled her beautiful lips taut. Her vulnerability was tearing Booker apart.

Booker was about to slide into the seat behind Jade's when squealing tires jump-started a rush of adrenaline. He looked up to see a nondescript compact car barely miss the delivery truck as it flew toward them.

His gaze registered the glint of metal extending from the driver's window. With one hand, he shoved the valet to the ground. With the other he pushed Jade into the car.

He fell on top of her just as the deafening crack of repeated gunshots, ricocheting bullets and shattering glass ruptured the relative quiet.

Booker pressed into the seat to push himself off Jade. His finger got tangled in her hair. When he worked it loose, his hand was dripping warm, sticky blood.

Chapter Thirteen

"Call 911," Booker ordered, struggling to keep a cool head. "Jade's been hit."

"No. I'm fine," Jade said, "except for my left shoulder that got shoved into the gearshift."

"I damn near lost a finger," Boros said. He lifted his bloody hand for them to see the ugly wound. Booker breathed easier as he realized that the blood that coated Jade's hair wasn't hers. Nor was it from a life-threatening injury.

Booker sprang from the car, this time with his pistol drawn, though the shooter wasn't likely to risk another drive-by attempt. For all the shooter knew, he'd hit his mark and they were all dead or near it.

The young valet was nowhere in sight, but Booker quickly spotted him scooting headfirst from beneath the front bumper. He appeared unhurt, though his face was vampire pale and the hood and right front fender of the car had both caught bullets.

"Man, that was close." The valet brushed off his pants and looked from Booker to the damaged bumper and hood. "If you hadn't shoved me to the ground when you did, I'd be dead."

"You having enough sense to squirm under the car didn't hurt, either. Are you hurt at all?"

"Skinned elbows from scooting under the car so fast." He stared at Booker's gun. "Did you get him?"

"Afraid not. It happened so fast I didn't even get off a shot."

"Do you think he'll be back?"

"Not likely, at least not anytime soon."

A siren sounded.

"Much less likely now," Booker said.

"Wait until the other valet hears about this. He's gonna go agro that he missed out on the excitement."

That was one way of putting a positive spin on the incident. Booker walked over to the driver's-side door.

Jade was leaning over Boros, examining his wound. "It's a glass cut," she said. "Bleeding has almost stopped, but it needs to be cleaned and bandaged."

"I put my hand up to protect my face when the shooting started."

"Better your finger than an eye," Jade said.

A squad car pulled up and stopped behind Boros's car. Two officers got out and took a quick look at the car before walking up to Booker.

"What happened here?" the taller one asked.

Boros burst into a heated explanation of the drive-by shooting, demanding a full police report.

The officers kept asking questions.

"If you want to know who's behind the shooting, I suggest you talk to Detective Winston Fielding," Boros said. "In fact, give me a minute, and I'll get him on the phone."

Boros made the call and wasted no time filling in the detective and blaming him for the incident.

"If you'd arrested Quaid Vaquero's real killer by now instead of trying to frame an innocent victim, things would never have gone this far. We could have been killed."

Booker could only hear one side of the discussion,

but he had no trouble filling in the conversation blanks for himself.

"There is positively no way you are questioning my client about anything, not even the weather, without my being present. You'll just have to wait until the police are through here and my finger is checked out. I expect a full investigation into the shooting in broad daylight…

"Fine. Come on over. You should see this for yourself. In the meantime, you can chat with the investigating officers."

Boros handed the phone to the nearest cop.

"Let's go inside so I can at least wash my wound. Winston Fielding is on his way. He can deal with this."

"I wish to God I'd never gone to Quaid's hotel suite that night," Jade said. "I wish I'd never laid eyes on that necklace. If not, Quaid might still be alive and none of this would be happening."

"You can't blame the violence on the necklace and certainly not on yourself," Boros said, "but it would definitely help if we could locate it and remove any doubt about you. Unfortunately, losing my temper on the phone just now probably didn't help matters with Fielding."

"Or maybe it did," Booker said. "Sometimes it takes an explosion to get the proper respect." That, he did know from experience.

BY THE TIME they reached NYPD headquarters, Jade's full-blown anger had returned. She'd been kidnapped. Her apartment had been wrecked. Now she could add being shot at to the list. If that weren't bad enough, Booker, Boros and even the valet's life had been in harm's way.

Enough was enough.

As she'd expected, Booker was not allowed to be pres-

ent for the questioning. Boros assured him he'd call when the interview concluded.

She and John Boros followed Detective Fielding through a maze of cubicles, most empty but some with plainclothes detectives typing reports, going through files or chatting with people standing around their desks.

Every one of them looked up as she passed. Normally, she didn't mind garnering a few admiring looks from the opposite sex. Knowing what these people were thinking about her, she'd much prefer being ignored.

Her mind skipped ahead and she wondered what she was really walking into. A good cop–bad cop routine? Being harassed in one of those boxlike, intimidating interrogation rooms that they always showed in TV police dramas? Or were they headed straight to the booking room where they'd take a mug shot, fingerprint her and toss her into a locked cell?

To her surprise, it was none of the above. Fielding took them to what looked like a conference room with semi-comfortable chairs and a long table. He took a seat opposite her and Fielding.

"Can I get you something? Coffee? Water?"

"Bourbon would be more appropriate after the morning we had," Boros said, "but water will do."

Fielding left them alone and returned a minute later with three waters. He opened his and gulped down half the bottle.

He'd never made it to the scene of the crime. Instead, he'd called Boros back, claimed something had come up and that he'd see the pictures and the police report later.

Fielding's face was square, his hairline already receding, though judging from his other features she'd guess him to be still in his forties. His stern expression seemed to be set in cement.

"If you have questions about your rights, ask your attorney. Other than that, I'll be asking the questions."

Definitely not playing the good cop.

Fielding dived into the interrogation process. "How long have you known Mack Lassiter?"

The question surprised her. "Is Mack a suspect in Quaid's murder?"

"You forgot rule one. I ask the questions."

So that was how it was going to be. "I've worked with Effacy Corporate Event Planning for three years. Ever since I've been there, we've used Mack's company to provide our security services."

"So basically you've known him for three years."

"Yes, but on a professional basis only. We're not friends."

"But you and Reggie are friends?"

"Absolutely not. I'd never seen him anywhere except at events where he was working security for his brother's company. But I know him now. He's a deranged—"

"You can vent later. Right now let's stick to the facts. Was your relationship with Quaid Vaquero strictly business?"

"Yes." That bordered on lying. "At least I thought it was business when he asked me to stop by his hotel suite the night of his murder. When I got there, it seemed more personal."

"Are you saying he made a move on you?" Fielding pushed.

"I'm not sure. His actions seemed a bit seductive, but his heritage is different than ours. He may just have been being nice since it was his last night before flying back to Barcelona."

"And the night you planned to kill him and steal the necklace?"

"Objection." Boros protested, his tone gruff and commanding. "That was an accusation, not a question. Do not respond to it, Jade." Jade struggled to tamp down her irritation, but she was all too aware things were not going well. "We can do this all day and I won't admit guilt, because I'm innocent. I had nothing to do with Quaid's murder or the theft of the necklace."

"Jade came in willing to explain what happened that night," Boros said. "I suggest you let her do that."

"Then you take it from here, Jade," Fielding said. "Tell me exactly what happened the night of Vaquero's murder. The truth."

"I *always* tell the truth." Unfortunately, she had only fuzzy memories surrounding the actual murder.

"In that case, I assume that neither you nor your attorney has a problem with my taping your explanation."

"It's fine with me," Jade said.

"As long as we stop taping anytime I say," Boros qualified.

"Let me ask a couple of nonaccusing questions to set up the interview and then you'll be free to give your account." Fielding leaned over and switched on a cell phone–sized recorder that sat near his elbow.

"Jade Dalton, according to your boss, Ruth Stevens, at Effacy Corporate Event Planning, you were in charge of coordinating Mr. Vaquero's private showing of his jewelry collection the night he was killed."

"I was in charge of all his events while Mr. Vaquero was in the States. All of which went off without a hint of complications until the last one."

Fielding nodded. "Tell me exactly what you remember of that night."

Jade began with Quaid's unveiling the expensive necklace that should have been under lock and key. As she talked, the scene came alive in her mind and the grief surrounding Quaid's death took hold once more.

Fielding didn't interrupt until she got to the part about room service arriving with champagne compliments of an unidentified donor.

He had her describe the man who served the champagne, asking several times for more details. She tried, but her recollection was sketchy at best. She'd been concentrating on Quaid and the exquisite cascade of diamonds and emeralds at the time.

The next bombardment of questions came when she told him about being kidnapped and handcuffed to the iron bed. He actually reached across the table and rolled a finger over the bruises and indentations where the metal had cut into her wrists.

He gave no indication that he believed or disbelieved her. The guy was probably a whiz at poker.

Strangely, the more she talked the more relieved she felt. She'd done nothing wrong. As number three used to say, "Don't judge the round of cheese you can't see by the mold on top." Reggie was the mold, but that didn't mean she couldn't trust Winston Fielding.

But then number three had been fired from one hotel restaurant for giving a dozen guests food poisoning, so maybe his advice wasn't that worthy after all.

"Why didn't you contact the police the minute you escaped Reggie Lassiter?"

"Because I was literally scared out of my wits. All I could think of was getting away from Reggie. I was afraid calling the police would somehow tip him off to finding me."

"That's not how we work around here."

"Isn't it? Leaks from your department have half the

reporters in the country speculating that I killed Quaid, stole the costly necklace and went on the run.

"And you certainly can't deny that I was right to run from Reggie. He tried to kill me again this morning and came within a few inches of succeeding. He might have killed John Boros, Booker and a young valet, as well."

The words had tumbled from her lips like water rushing over a dam. Reggie Lassiter had made her life a living nightmare and she wouldn't let Fielding make it sound as if she were overreacting.

"If you have any concrete evidence to disprove Jade's account, let's hear it," Boros said.

The detective leaned toward Jade, his eyes searing into hers. Her confidence took a nosedive.

"If I buy your story that Reggie murdered Quaid for the necklace, then why did he kidnap you?"

"I told you. He thinks I have the necklace."

"If you don't have it, do you have any idea who does?"

"Objection," Boros said again. "She told you she was wasn't involved in the theft. It's your job to find out who was, not hers."

Jade bit back the frustration that was building to a crescendo again. This time it was the situation more than the questioning that upset her.

"Maybe the drowned man you found beneath the Lassiters' deck had the necklace," she said. "Perhaps Lassiter killed him for it."

"If that's the case, there would be no reason for Reggie to be still coming after you?"

Jade had to admit the situation did not look good for her. "All I can say for certain is that I'm innocent," Jade said for what seemed like the tenth time. "I do not have the necklace. I have never had the necklace except for the few minutes I wore it before I was drugged. I've been kidnapped, tormented, had my apartment and everything in it ruined and now I've been shot at. If you want to arrest me, I can't stop you, but Quaid's killer will still be on the loose."

"The whole damn country is demanding your arrest," Fielding said.

Boros banged a fist on the table. "If you arrest her, you damn well better have the evidence to back it up, or I promise you this is going to backfire on you."

"I'm damned if I do and damned if I don't," Fielding said. "All I'm after is the truth."

The detective took out his phone and made a call. A couple of minutes later, a woman in her NYPD blues came in, handed him a folder and left again.

He opened the file and spread a dozen mug shots across the table between them. "Jade, I want you to take a look and see if you recognize any of these men."

Jade took her time, examining each photo thoroughly, though not sure who she was looking for. She was over halfway through the photos when she found it. Recognition was instant, but she studied the mug shot a few seconds longer just to be sure.

"That's him." Jade pushed the photo back toward Fielding. "That's the room-service guy who uncorked, poured and obviously drugged the champagne."

"Are you certain?"

"I am, unless he has a twin."

"He doesn't."

Boros stretched his neck for a better look. "Have you arrested him?"

"No, and I won't be. It was his body found beneath the dock where Jade was allegedly held hostage."

"No need to say more," Boros quipped. "He and Reggie were in this together. Reggie took him out. Corpses never talk."

"So, where do we go from here?" Jade asked.

Fielding turned off the recorder and then slid the mug shots back into the folder. "The news tonight is going to crucify me, but I'm not going to arrest you, at least not yet."

The release of tension was so swift and so dramatic she felt as if her muscles were dissolving.

"I'm sticking my neck out for you, Jade."

"You're doing your job," Boros reminded him.

Fielding ignored Boros and kept his focus on Jade. "I need a few things from you in return."

"You want to negotiate with me, even though I'm innocent?"

"No. I want solid reasons to give my boss for not arresting you. I'd like you to voluntarily give me a DNA sample and take a lie-detector test."

Boros put up a hand as if he didn't want to hear more. "After what Jade's been through at the hands of an NYPD officer, you guys ought to be jumping through hoops hoping to keep her from suing."

"All I'm asking for is justice," Jade said. "I'll be glad to do both. Maybe that will quiet the news hustlers."

"Don't count on that," Boros said. "When they get a story like this, they ride that horse until it dies."

"I'd like you to stay in town a few days so that the NYPD can provide 24/7 protection," Fielding continued.

"I have a bodyguard," Jade said.

"The Navy SEAL who was with you when you were shot at?"

"Right. Booker Knox."

"As long as that's your call."

"It's my call. If he decides he's had enough, I'll let you know."

"Is that it?" Boros asked.

"Not quite."

Jade had the distinct impression that the worst was yet to come. Fielding's next request convinced her she was right.

CERTAIN HE'D GO crazy if he tried to sit in the precinct drinking stale coffee and worrying about what was going on with Jade for the next couple of hours, Booker decided to take a taxi back to the hotel where they'd stayed last night, pick up the few belongings they had with them and move them to a new hotel.

The most likely scenario for the shooter's knowing where to find them this morning was that he'd watched them leave her apartment last night, followed them to the hotel and then to Boros's office this morning. That was a case of serious stalking.

When the enemy retreated, he was probably just re-grouping and reloading, Murphy's Law. No reason to make it easy on Lassiter.

Booker went back to the precinct, waited around a few minutes for the call from Boros that didn't come and then stepped back outside. He started walking west. It was not his first time in Manhattan, but still, crowded sidewalks, honking horns and the food carts lining the streets always made him feel as if he'd stepped into a different world.

Everything moved faster here. Even street vendors had no patience if you took too much time making up your mind about what you wanted on your pretzel or hot dog. Cars and especially taxis sped from one traffic jam to the next. Shoppers bustled in and out of stores.

He could definitely see Jade thriving in a city like this.

The theater. Fashion. Concerts. Museums. Conventions. Wall Street. Banking. This was the hub of happenings.

A terrific city if you were a corporate event planner. Meeting famous people like Quaid Vaquero as well as the movers and shakers in the business world was probably commonplace to Jade.

A great city, but not for him. But then, how many would volunteer for the life he had chosen? His missions had taken him into some of the most desolate, miserable and volatile places on earth.

He wouldn't keep doing that forever, but he wasn't ready to give it up yet. He'd trained too hard for it. He was good at what he did. He served his country and saved lives. He made a difference and he did it working with the best bunch of guys on earth.

When he did give it up, he could see himself settling in an area like Oak Grove, Texas. Maybe even on a small ranch of his own. Rivers for fishing. Woods for hunting. Trails for horseback riding. A place where kids get out and run and play and...

Kids. Where the hell did that come from? He could fight terrorists, even given the rules of engagements he had to work with in today's world, but kids? He'd have no idea where to start.

On the other hand, Cannon Dalton was a great dad and he'd been a bull rider.

Finally, Booker's phone vibrated. His throat grew desert dry as he checked the caller ID. The apprehension turned to disappointment when he realized it wasn't Boros.

Zoe again, or at least someone calling from the same number. It wouldn't be for him, but he decided to take the call, anyway.

"Hello."

He could hear breathing but no response.

"Zoe, this is Booker Knox, a good friend of Jade's. She isn't available to take your call, but I know she's eager to hear from you. Can I give her a message?"

More seconds of silence passed before the connection went dead. Jade would be disappointed, but Booker didn't see how Zoe could offer much in the way of help with the investigation when she'd been in Barcelona at the time of the murder.

He walked for an hour, absently staring into store windows and dodging turning cars at intersections while his thoughts focused on the missing necklace. Only one thing was certain in his mind, Jade did not have it.

But even if you believed she did, why try to kill her as someone had this morning? Not much chance of getting a necklace from a corpse.

Unless this morning's shooter had been an excellent marksman and had intended to frighten, not kill, her. Or if he'd wanted to get to her before she spilled her guts to the police. Either way, she was still in danger.

Booker passed a café with outdoor seating that had a couple of empty tables. The sign said seat yourself, so he took a table next to the sidewalk. A pigeon dropped by to steal a bread crumb left by the previous diner.

When the waitress arrived, Booker took a quick look at the menu and ordered coffee and a Reuben sandwich with fries. The coffee arrived quickly. Hot. Strong. Black. And really good.

He sipped and went back to searching for the missing element in the case of the necklace. His sandwich arrived just as his phone vibrated again. The same nervous knot balled in his throat. Again, the call was not Boros with news of how things were going for Jade.

"Any news?" R.J. asked once they'd passed the greeting stage.

"Still waiting."

"I don't know if you've caught the news today, but things have taken a turn for the worse."

"How's that?"

"They're saying that the police have not been able to locate Reggie Lassiter. They're speculating that Jade and Reggie were in on the murder together and that Reggie has left the country with the necklace and Jade is going to pin everything on him and then when things die down, she'll join him."

"Some reporter probably stayed up all night dreaming that one up," Booker said. "But they still have it all wrong."

"I reckon. But the NYPD must be under powerful pressure to arrest Jade."

Apparently, R.J. hadn't heard about the morning's drive-by shooting. Booker decided not to fill him in. The old man had enough to deal with, and Booker didn't want to cause him any more stress.

"Travis and Faith flew back in this morning on an early flight," R.J. said. "He's touching base with a detective friend who works for the NYPD to see what he can find out about the case."

"The Daltons do seem to have friends in high places."

"And I have a few in low places," R.J. said, "just in case we ever need one of them."

Booker had no doubt that he was serious. "Let's stick with the high places for now."

"I talked to my banker this morning," R.J. said. "He says if we need bail money he can have it for me in a few minutes' notice."

"Good. I hope it doesn't come to that, but nice to know the money's there if needed."

"Yeah, well, I don't want Jade locked up with a bunch of criminals."

"I second that."

"I know she was raised on concrete and likes living that way, but if she doesn't get arrested, we've got plenty of room right here at the Dry Gulch for both of you. Nice place to get your head screwed on straight again after it's been knocked off-kilter."

"No place I'd rather be right now," Booker said truthfully. "By the way, Jade had another offer of help last night."

"From her mother?"

"No, but she has talked to Kiki. Her mother gives tons of advice that Jade promptly ignores. It seems to work for them. It was your son Jake who called."

"Well, dog bite my buttons. He's finally showing a little family spirit. I knew he couldn't be his mother's son and not have some heart in him. What did Jade tell him?"

"She hasn't talked to him yet. She had a message from him on her phone when we got back to her apartment last night."

"I want to do something to help, Booker. It don't have to be something big, but I've been a no-show all her life. I want to show up this time. Put her up in a nice, safe hotel. Treat her like a princess. Cost don't matter."

"I might just take you up on that, R.J., and I'll be sure to let her know that you're providing the funds and that you really want to help."

"I appreciate that. Call me the second you hear from her. We're all on pins and needles here."

They talked a minute more. Booker might feel differently about R.J. if he was in Jade's shoes. But R.J. wasn't his MIA dad. Booker hadn't known the old rounder during his drinking, gambling and womanizing days. He only knew the R.J. who was dying and just thankful to have his family around him every day God gave him.

Booker liked him a lot. Jade might, too, if she gave the man half a chance.

He'd almost finished his sandwich when he got the call he'd been waiting on.

"You can meet us back at the precinct anytime," Boros said. "Jade's ready to go."

Mere words had never sounded better to Booker's ear.

"So that's it with the police?"

"No. Jail is off the table for now, but not the trouble. Jade will tell you about it when you get here."

Not particularly comforting, but she'd be in Booker's bed tonight instead of a jail cell. How bad could the rest be?

Chapter Fourteen

Jade stopped just outside the precinct door and took a deep breath. "I need a drink, something stronger than a diet soda this time."

"I can handle that," Booker said. "How about joining us for a celebratory drink, Mr. Boros?"

"Thanks, but I'll have to take a rain check this time. I've got too much work waiting for me back at the office and I want to check with the body shop about my car."

"I can't tell you how much I appreciate what you've done so far," Jade said. "I never realized how important having the right attorney is until you stood by me with Fielding and let him know he couldn't barrel right over me."

He smiled. "That's what I get the big bucks for. But don't shortchange yourself. You held your own in there. Let me know when you're scheduled for the lie-detector test."

Booker frowned. "Did you volunteer for that?"

"Why not? I have nothing to hide."

Booker turned to Boros. "Isn't it possible to get a false negative on those?"

"The accuracy does depend to some extent on the person administering the test," Boros explained. "I'll make sure Jade gets someone who's had lots of experience."

"I'm not sweating the test," Jade assured him. "The reenactment is another story."

"What reenactment? I'm lost," Booker said.

"I'll explain it all over a drink," Jade assured him.

"One last question," Boros said. "Leif is expecting a call from me to hear how things went this morning."

"I think the whole Dalton clan is awaiting that call," Booker said.

"Do I have your authorization to discuss it with him, Jade?"

"Do I have a choice in the matter?"

"Attorney-client privilege is still at play here. I have a form in my briefcase that I'll need you to sign if you agree to his being part of the team."

"How about Travis and Brit?" Booker asked. "Shouldn't they be part of the team, as well?"

"Leif can use them as research participants without formal approval."

"Then I definitely think you should sign the form," Booker said.

"Fine. I'll sign. Like it or not, I seem to have become part of the family."

"You could have it a lot worse," Boros said.

He nodded toward a black town car that had just pulled up in front of the police station with the same young law-school-intern driver who'd dropped them off earlier.

"That's my ride. Step over there with me, and we can take care of everything in a matter of seconds."

Once done, Booker reached out to shake Boros's hand. "When do we see you again?"

"I'll be with Jade every step of the way, including the lie-detector test. Fielding knows he is not to talk to her about anything without my being present. Hopefully, our next meeting won't include the excitement of gunfire."

"I'd feel a lot better about those chances if Reggie Lassiter was behind bars," Jade said.

"I expect that to be at any moment," Boros said. "In the meantime, Booker, watch over Jade."

Boros's tone grew more serious. "I know you're more capable and experienced than any bodyguard we could hire. But you're up against a guy who's already murdered and kidnapped."

"Got it. Nothing's more dangerous than an enemy with nothing to lose."

"If you ever feel the need for added security, Detective Fielding has promised to provide it. Don't hesitate to ask."

"I won't," Booker assured him. "I'm here to protect Jade, not play hero."

Booker put a hand to the small of her back as they walked away from Boros. Heated awareness zinged through her. Never had a man's casual touch affected her the way Booker's did. Part of the giddy pleasure surely came from knowing she wasn't about to be arrested, but some of it was just the thrill of Booker.

"I had a lot of time to scope out the area," Booker said. "There's a neat-looking bar a couple of blocks from here. We can sit inside and find a quiet corner where you can tell me all I missed."

"Sounds perfect. Do they also have food? I'm dangerous when I drink on an empty stomach."

"You're dangerous when you aren't drinking, Jade Dalton. But they do have food."

In minutes, they were seated at the table Booker had requested. In the far-right corner where he took the chair with its back against a wall providing him an unobstructed view of the front door.

He always seemed low-key, never made her feel as if bullets were going to start flying at her any minute. Yet she had no doubt he was in full control. He'd proved it this morning, shoving the valet to the ground and covering her body with his. And that had been with only a split second's warning.

Boros might not be quite as convinced of Booker's lifeguarding abilities as she was. Come to think of it, that could be why he'd turned down Booker's offer to join them for a drink. Hanging out with Jade was practically suicide.

She went over the interview in her mind, pulling together the facts she needed to share with Booker as they waited for their order. When the waitress returned with the drinks, Booker proposed a toast.

She shuddered as memories of Quaid's toast a few nights ago crept into her mind. The future had loomed before him them. A few minutes later, he was dead.

If just a toast disturbed her this much, what Fielding wanted of her would be traumatic.

Still, she lifted her martini glass, ready to clink it with Booker's icy mug of beer.

"To an afternoon of joyous perfection," he said.

"I'll drink to that." She wasn't going to count on it, but if anyone could make it happen, it would be Booker.

"Now for the details," Booker said. "You know I'm dying to hear everything."

They settled into the conversation as they sipped their drinks.

"To start with, the interrogation wasn't quite what I expected. Detective Fielding is a smooth operator. He can lure you into thinking you're having a casual chat and then slam you with a whammy. He made accusations that had me convinced he was on the verge of arresting me right until the point he said he wasn't—not *yet*."

"So he hasn't taken arrest totally off the table?"

"No, but he listened attentively when I told him about the kidnapping experience. That was the one thing I don't think he was expecting."

Booker reached across the table and slid his hand over hers. "An experience gruesome enough to make a super-hero panic and run."

"Not in Fielding's mind, but that's okay. Believing in my innocence was the important thing."

She told Booker about the mug shots and her instant recognition of the room-service waiter in one of the photos. "Fielding admitted that was also the man they found beneath the dock."

"Then it logically follows that he was also one of the three men you saw in the room after you were drugged. He's dead. That leaves only Reggie and one other of Quaid's killers alive. Did Fielding give any indication that they've identified him?"

"No. He wouldn't even give me the name of the dead man."

"Really? That should be public knowledge. If it's not, I'm sure your brother Travis can get that for you. He and his wife are back at the ranch now."

"How do you know that?"

"R.J. called. He's worried about you."

"Well, gee. Guess that explains it. If I'd had run-ins with the law growing up, I might have had a father."

"He knows he's made mistakes, Jade."

"Funny how that doesn't change the past."

The waitress delivered the hummus, pita and olive appetizer she'd ordered. Jade spread the creamy dip on a triangle of pita and nibbled, irritated with herself for reacting to Booker's comment the way she had.

"Sorry for the sarcasm. I just find all this sudden fake-father love a little hard to swallow."

"You don't have to justify your feelings about R.J. to me. Let's get back to your meeting with Detective Fielding. Is there anything else I should know?"

The one thing she'd agreed to that she was already regretting. "Fielding wants to re-create the scene in Quaid's hotel suite the night of the murder."

"So that's the reenactment you mentioned. How is that supposed to help? You were so groggy you can't even identify who was in the room."

"Fielding didn't explain his motive, but I have the feeling it's more connected to locating the missing necklace than to discovering the facts surrounding the murder. I told him I was wearing it when the champagne was poured. It stands to reason one of the attackers took it."

"Unless it disappeared between the time you became groggy and the thieves broke in."

"Quaid and I were the only ones there."

"The only ones you *know* were there. I've given this a lot of thought this morning and come up with some scenarios that aren't quite so black-and-white."

"Meaning?"

"Quaid might have arranged for someone to slip in and take the necklace while you were too dazed to notice."

"Why would he steal his own necklace?"

"Maybe it was an insurance scam. He could collect on the stolen necklace and then reuse the diamonds and emeralds in another creation. Or it could be that the jewels were inferior and he had an overinflated appraisal that would allow him to make a bundle on an insurance claim."

"I'm not an expert, but the necklace was more exquisite than anything I'd ever seen. I find it hard to believe the jewels were inferior quality or fake."

"I'm just considering all options, trying to think out-side the box, since we haven't gotten anywhere inside it."

"If you're on the right track, it would mean I totally misjudged Quaid. And if it was his plan, something would have had to go terribly wrong for Quaid to end up dead."

Booker finished his beer.

"Maybe Fielding is right and my reenacting what I remember of the night will stir a repressed memory," Jade said.

"It will definitely bring the murder and kidnapping back to front and center in your mind. I hate to see you keep reliving this."

"I'll keep reliving it until we have the full story even without the role-playing."

"I want to be there for the reenactment, Jade."

"It's a crime scene. I'm not sure the detective will ap-prove."

"Tell him I go or you don't."

Booker made it sound so easy, but he was used to calling the shots and so was Detective Fielding. She se-riously doubted a power struggle between them would work to her favor.

"I'll ask Fielding," she promised. That was the best she could do.

"When is this reenactment supposed to take place?"

"Fielding said he'd call me when he got it set up. He warned it might be on short notice."

"With luck, it won't be tonight. You deserve a break. How about another drink?" Booker asked.

"No, thanks, but you can order one if you like. I'm going to try to get down a few more bites of food before we go back to the hotel."

"About that, we won't be going back. I canceled our

reservation for tonight. I don't trust Reggie not to make another attempt on your life. I made us a reservation at a hotel near Central Park under a fake name so hopefully he won't discover your whereabouts."

"You Navy SEALs think of everything."

"And look cool doing it. A little unknown part of the SEAL creed. Oh, I almost forgot with all of your news, but you had another call from Zoe while you were with Fielding."

"What did she say?"

"Nothing. I answered, told her you weren't available and urged her to leave a message, but she broke the connection."

"Call her back for me, please. I have to find out why she seems so desperate to see me yet didn't call back last night."

Booker punched in Zoe's number and handed Jade the phone. This time Zoe answered on the first ring.

"Hi, Zoe. It's Jade. We got disconnected last night, but I'm free right now if you still want to get together."

"Yes. We need to talk. Now is good."

"Where are you staying?"

"Near the big store. Macy's. On Thirty-Fourth Street."

"It would be difficult to talk in a department store. How about a coffee shop? There's one nearby."

"No. Better in Macy's. With the perfumes. Like you don't know me."

This was sounding more clandestine by the second. "Zoe, are you afraid to be seen with me?"

"You are wanted by the police."

That explained it. Zoe didn't want to be connected with the woman suspected of killing her employer. Good thinking, since if anyone saw them together they might snap a picture that could go virile on YouTube before they left the store.

"I was questioned by the police this morning," Jade assured her. "I wasn't arrested. The police are no longer looking for me."

"Act like you don't know me," Zoe persisted. "I'm wearing black pants and a plain white shirt."

"What time?"

"In twenty minutes."

"I'll be there," Jade promised.

"You're meeting her in a department store?" Booker questioned when she broke the connection. "What's that about?"

"It appears what she's afraid of being seen with me. She doesn't want anyone to think we're actually out together. I have a killer reputation. Ready for a stroll?"

"If I have to go shopping, does it have to be in the perfume department? I hate being ambushed and sprayed with the scent of bucks and hippopotamus tusks."

"Where would you prefer to do your spying?"

"Lingerie is nice."

"We can try that after we leave Zoe. As thanks for saving my life this morning, you can pick out anything you want to take off me tonight."

"We can start naked and save you money and me time. And who said anything about waiting until tonight?"

ZOE WAS WEARING black pants and a white shirt, but she was anything but inconspicuous. Straight black hair fell past her shoulders, so shiny it glimmered even in the indoor lighting. Her dark eyes were doe-like, her complexion smooth as porcelain. Even Quaid's collection of gorgeous models would have a hard time competing with her beauty. Quaid had never mentioned how stunning she was.

Still, Jade had no doubt she was looking at the right woman. The quick nervous glances gave her away. Zoe would surely recognize Jade, since she'd obviously watched enough of the TV coverage to know she didn't want to be seen with Jade.

Jade meandered Zoe's way and stopped at the gift display next to where she was standing. Jade picked up the lotion sample and squirted a few drops on her hand, rubbing it in thoroughly.

Zoe looked around again. So did Jade. The clerks were all busy with actual customers. No one was paying them any attention. So much for her dubious notoriety. When women shopped, they were on another planet.

"Thanks for coming," Zoe whispered. "I wish our meeting could have been with Quaid. He was so fond of you."

"I enjoyed working with him very much. I know how hard his death must be for you."

"Yes," Zoe said. "Tragic to die so young, but that's not why I asked you to meet me."

"Why are you here?"

"You can't keep the necklace, Jade. Quaid trusted you."

Not this again. "Last night you said you believed in my innocence."

"I know you did not kill Quaid. But I also know that he wanted you to wear the necklace for his final showing. He was trying hard to impress you."

"I tried on the necklace. That's all. It was never in my possession. I'm not a thief. If I had it, I would have given it to the police."

"No. Not the police." Zoe's voice rose with a new

urgency. She quickly lowered it again. "You must give it to me. It belongs to the estate."

"A moot point, Zoe. I don't have it."

"It is very dangerous to keep it, Jade. It is cursed. Quaid died because of it. You must not make that mistake."

"Quaid didn't die of a curse, Zoe. He died because of a very wicked man who will soon be locked away in prison. But even he doesn't have the necklace."

"I know that you have it, Jade. You must give it back. Quaid would want *me* to have it."

Perhaps Jade had misread the fear factor and it was grief and perhaps a touch of unwarranted jealousy that was tearing Zoe apart. Or perhaps she was worried about how she would make a living without Quaid or that she'd lose her home.

Whatever the reason, she wanted the necklace so desperately, but Jade couldn't help her. "The police are working to find the necklace and the man who murdered Quaid, Zoe. It's in their hands now. You should take Quaid's body and go back to Barcelona. You'll feel better there."

"You are making a terrible mistake, Jade." Eyes downcast, Zoe turned and walked away.

TRUE TO JADE'S WORD, they had gone shopping for lingerie and Booker had picked out a black lace negligee that had gotten him so turned on right there in the store he was still practically panting.

She'd bought a few pair of panties as well, lacy scraps that would barely cover her triangle of rich red hair. And one black bra. One was all she needed, she'd assured him, for special occasions.

Then they'd hit the dress department. He'd sat in an

uncomfortable chair while she paraded her choices for his opinion, or so she claimed. More likely, she liked seeing him drool.

He'd voted for a slinky black dress that showed just the right amount of cleavage to drive a man to distraction and had a flirty-tailed skirt that accentuated her dynamite legs. She'd bought that, a yellow polka-dot number that curved around her shapely hips and an emerald-green two-piece suit, still sexy but with a professional edge.

It might have been a typical afternoon of shopping except that Booker knew Jade was faking much of the playful, sexy mood. She was bothered by Zoe's situation and the fact that Reggie Lassiter was still free to walk the streets.

Booker was running on automatic now, his eyes constantly on the lookout for problems, his muscles on ready, his mind-set geared toward protection.

"These should do until I get a chance to see if any of my other clothes are salvageable," Jade said as the clerk fit them into a plastic hanging bag.

"Does that mean we can head to the hotel?"

"Not without shoes."

"You're wearing shoes."

"These are walking shoes."

"What else are you planning to do in your shoes?"

"Turn you on."

"You can do that just by showing up."

She tried on several pairs while he watched, admired and groaned. All of them looked like instruments of foot torture with heels high enough to break an ankle if she fell.

"These or these?" she asked, holding one pair in her hand and pointing at the ones on her feet.

They were both a burnished gold. One was shinier,

but other than that, he couldn't tell a dime's worth of difference. They both looked fantastic on her.

"From a man's point of view, I'd say go with the one that feels the best."

"Looks, Booker. It's all about the look."

"Then buy them both."

"That's what I'm thinking," she said, "except I'll take the patent in black."

"Patent in black," he quipped. "Isn't that a movie title?"

"It might be after tonight."

"You wicked vamp. Get the shoes and let's get out of here."

"Yes, sir."

By the time they hit the streets again, traffic had picked up to the point he no longer had to worry about a drive-by. Nobody was moving, but that didn't stop the drivers from laying on their horns.

"Shall we walk?" Jade asked "Or would you rather spend the next half hour going two blocks in a taxi?"

"Unless you want to neck, let's walk."

Two blocks later, he spotted a man weaving in and out of a crowd of pedestrians and racing toward them. Booker steeled his body, ready to wrestle the man to the sidewalk if he went for a gun or tried to assault Jade.

And then he spotted the man's camera, one large enough it should have had wheels.

Flashes popped and an instant later the man ran away even faster than he'd approached.

"My first paparazzi attack," Jade said. "Now I see why actors and actresses abhor them."

"Yeah," Booker agreed. "The Dry Gulch Ranch would sure look good about now."

"I never thought I'd say it, but I agree."

BOOKER LAY ACROSS the bed in his boxers, more sexually satiated than he'd ever been in his life. In ordinary circumstances Jade's self-confident, fun-loving attitude toward making love and toward life in general would be impressive. Take into account what she was going through now and the attitude was awing.

If that weren't enough, she was also gorgeous, spunky and competent enough at her job that she'd been put in charge of Quaid Vaquero's business agenda while he was in the States, even though she couldn't be much over twenty years old.

The mystery was why she seemed as crazy about him as he was about her. He figured it had to do with his taking on the role of bodyguard. When she no longer needed protection, she'd likely dump him fast. And he'd return to his unit with memories and images in his head that would keep any woman from ever measuring up to Jade.

He watched as she tugged the slinky black dress over her shapely hips and onto her shoulders.

She gave an extra wiggle as she turned and made a face at him. "Are you going to get dressed for dinner or not?"

"I'm having too much fun watching you."

"Then get out of bed and zip me up."

He slid off the bed, walked over and zipped the dress slowly, loving the feel of his fingers against her silky-smooth skin. Once the dress was zipped and snapped, he couldn't resist a couple of nibbles at her earlobe.

"Dinner reservations in twenty minutes," she reminded him playfully. "They don't have a dress code, but I'm pretty sure boxers would get you kicked out."

"Really? You New Yorkers are such sticklers about your wardrobe." Reluctantly, he pulled on his navy trousers. It wasn't just the scenery that he hated to leave, it was the comforting security of being locked in their own private space.

But tonight, he'd minimized the risks while giving Jade a chance to dress up and celebrate her freedom.

He'd booked a private alcove in the hotel's dining room, one where they could enjoy the atmosphere and the music and even dance on their private dance floor if they wanted. He'd been assured that the waiters serving them had been with the restaurant for years and were very reliable.

They'd waited on celebrities, politicians and even known Mafia heads. They were as good at or better at confidentiality than the best attorneys in the city.

Booker wanted no ugly surprises tonight.

He could never have pulled this off on his budget, but he gave R.J. a call and the old rancher had been eager to spring for the tab. More than eager, he'd been thankful he could help.

If Jade would give R.J. half a chance, Booker was sure she'd find something to like about him. She might not ever think of him as her dad, but he was sure R.J. would be thrilled with a lot less.

They were walking out the door when Booker's phone vibrated. He checked the caller ID. Damn. The timing could not be worse. "It's Detective Fielding and probably for you."

"I have to take it."

"I was afraid you'd say that."

He heard enough of the conversation to know that dinner would have to wait.

Chapter Fifteen

A chill settled in Jade's bones the second Detective Fielding slipped the plastic key card in the slot, turned the knob and opened the door to what had been Quaid's hotel suite. A crush of memories fought for control of her mind.

Quaid's fastening the clasp of the necklace. The light reflecting off the diamonds as if they were a heaven full of stars.

The feel of Quaid's caressing fingers on her skin. The sound of the cork popping on the expensive bottle of champagne. The sparkling bubbles inching up the crystal flute.

The helplessness as she'd crumpled to the floor.

Booker reached for her hand and squeezed it as if he could sense the crippling power of her emotions.

Surprisingly, Fielding had given in to Booker's request to be here without much of an argument. Two other police officers had joined them as well, another homicide detective named Hampton and a forensics specialist from the Crime Scene Unit Fielding simply referred to as Bones.

And, of course, Boros was there.

For once she wished she wasn't dressed to kill. It might make them see her as a seductress who'd lured Quaid to his death.

"This is the exact suite where the murder place took

place," Fielding said. "We've complied with the hotel's request not to put up any crime-scene tape that might scare off their other penthouse guests and they've agreed to leave this suite exactly as the first responders found it until we finish the investigation."

"I take it you're not counting Lassiter as a first responder," Bones said.

"No. He called in the crime, but he didn't even stick around until CSU got here and, as you know, he hasn't been seen or heard from since."

"He was seen and heard from," Boros reminded him quickly. "At the fishing camp the morning after and on the street this morning."

"Not seen or heard from by the police," Fielding corrected himself. He unsuccessfully tried to avoid stepping on the beach-ball-size bloodstains as he walked to the middle of the suite's living area.

"Look around you, Jade. Is this the way you remember it?"

Pillows from the tan sofa were scattered about the room. One lamp was overturned, as was a chair. The TV had been ripped from the wall. Every drawer had been yanked from the chest below the TV.

It was her apartment all over again minus the black spray paint that had likely completely ruined everything of value she owned.

"It's the same furnishings," Jade said, "but the last I remember of this room, it was fastidiously neat and clean with no bloodstains on the carpet."

"Then you have no memory of it looking like this?" Fielding asked.

"None."

"Were you in this room when Quaid first showed you the necklace?"

She hesitated, struggling to make sure the details were clear in her mind before answering.

"Yes. I don't remember being in the bedroom, except..."

Fielding waited without pushing her to finish the sentence. "I collapsed on the floor in here, but as I mentioned in your office, I vaguely remember Quaid picking me up and laying me down on a bed. I must have been in the bedroom then but not before that."

"Do you remember Mr. Vaquero touching you either appropriately or inappropriately after that?"

She saw where this was going and it was making her ill. "Quaid's not the one who had the date-rape drug added to my champagne. He wouldn't do anything like that. You're twisting the situation into perverse things that didn't happen."

"We're not intentionally twisting anything," Fielding said calmly. "We just need to find the truth in a very warped murder case."

"Why don't we get to the reenactment?" Bones said. "We'll stand back and let Ms. Dalton move us along at her pace."

"Without constant interruptions," Boros insisted.

Fielding pulled a cheap piece of costume jewelry from his jacket pocket and handed it to Jade. "I know we talked at length today, but for the benefit of Hampton and Bones here, I'd like you to walk and talk us through everything that happened the night of the murder."

"We're not expecting a theater performance," Hampton said, "but we'd like you to move around the room as you deem appropriate so that we can get a picture in our minds of what preceded the murder."

"Mostly so we can get some kind of clue what happened to that dratted necklace," Bones said. "You'd think it was the Holy Grail the way the media is carrying on."

"Where do I start?"

"How about with how you came to be in Vaquero's suite that night?" Hampton said. "Was it part of the usual routine on the night of a showing or was this something out of the ordinary? Unlike the newscasters going around saying everything that pops into their heads, we need to separate fact from conjecture."

"The fact is, that night was the first time I'd been to Quaid's suite. Before that, we'd met in my office or in the hotel restaurant to conduct business. That night I got a text from Quaid while I was on my way to the hotel for the showing. He asked me to drop by his suite first."

"But he didn't mention the necklace?"

"No, and I never guessed he'd keep something that costly anywhere but in a locked and protected safe or on guarded display. It was his last showing before flying back to Spain. We'd worked well together and his show-ings had been a tremendous success. I thought he just wanted to say thank-you before the evening got under way."

Uninterrupted, she dropped back into the scene as if she'd been hypnotized, barely realizing that she was sharing it with the others.

Quaid, so excited to show her what he'd referred to as the crown of his collection. The necklace that had been so striking it had stolen her breath away.

She lifted the chain of cheap painted stones Field-ing had provided and held it against her throat. "When Quaid fastened the exquisite cascade of diamonds and emeralds around my neck, he insisted I look at myself in the mirror."

She spun around. "The mirror is missing."

"What mirror?" Fielding asked.

"There was a full-size tilt mirror sitting right there." She pointed to a spot between the sofa and the window. "Dark wood. I remember thinking it looked antique but probably wasn't."

Bones walked to the door of the bedroom. "Are you talking about that mirror?"

She walked over so that she could see what he was referring to.

"That's it," she said. "But it wasn't in the bedroom. It was in the living area. I'm sure of it."

"Not in the photographs CSU took of the crime scene a few hours after the murder," Bones said. "I've studied them extensively. Vaquero's body was on the floor in the living area. The mirror was in the bedroom, just as it is now."

"Could it have been moved after Vaquero's murder?" Booker asked, though Fielding had warned him not to insinuate himself into tonight's discussion.

"Possibly, if someone had carried it around what would have been a pool of blood by then," Bones answered. "If they'd dragged it, it would have left a trail of blood."

"I'm sure it was in the living area," Jade repeated.

"Let's get back to the reenactment," Hampton said. "We can throw self-moving-mirror ideas around at the precinct."

Jade picked up where she left off, but this time she didn't dissolve into the story as she had before. She concentrated on details, leaving nothing out, including the earrings Quaid had given her as a gift and the fact that Reggie had admitted to taking them.

She didn't grow uneasy again until she came to the part where the drugs began to take effect.

"I became disoriented and felt as if I were floating through a heavy fog."

"Was Quaid reacting in the same way?" Bones asked.

"I don't know," she answered honestly. "I assumed later we'd both been drugged, but I can't say that for certain."

"But he was still functioning when you blacked out the first time?" Hampton questioned.

"He picked me up and carried me to the bed, or at least I think he did. I remember being in his arms and then he put me down. I thought I was in bed, but I suppose it could have been the sofa."

"Putting her on the bed would be consistent with the mussed bed," Bones said.

"Let's move to the bedroom," Hampton said. "We may as well do this right." They went through the door single file. Booker stuck close to her.

"Lie down on the bed, if you will," Fielding said. "I'd like to see what you can see of the living area from there."

She shook her head. "Not in this dress."

Bones and Hampton tried without succeeding to hide their knowing smiles. Booker gave her a thumbs-up.

"No problem," Fielding said. "I wasn't thinking."

"He's not quite human," Bones joked.

Fielding ignored the comment. "Stand by the bed and see what kind of view you have from there."

She obliged. "I can see the area where the biggest bloodstains are on the carpet. I can see the right half of the sofa. I can't see the area where the mirror was, nor can I see the front door."

Bones took out his cell phone and started punching keys. "I need to get that down before I forget."

"Tell Bones and Hampton what you saw and heard as you were drifting into unconsciousness."

"My legs kind of folded under me and I just crumpled to the floor. I think I may have reached out to Quaid for help. I remember he picked me up and carried me to his bed. The last thing I felt was his hands at my throat."

She stopped short, realizing the impact of what she'd just said. When she looked up, all four of the men were staring at her.

"I'd forgotten that," she said. "I'm not sure why I remembered it now."

"Revelations like that are what we're looking for," Fielding assured her. "Did he remove the necklace?"

"I have no idea. I think I must have blacked out then."

"Then what makes you so sure Reggie Lassiter was ever in this room?" Hampton asked.

"I must have come to for a few seconds. I remember hearing his voice."

"But not seeing him?"

"I saw three men. I'm almost certain one of them was Reggie. He appeared to float around the room with Quaid. I know this sounds crazy, but it's what I remember."

"Did you recognize the other men?"

"No, but I didn't see them up close. They were merely shadowy figures in the background. I wouldn't have recognized my best friend under those circumstances."

"Yet you're sure Reggie Lassiter was in the room?"

"I can't be positive. But I thought it was Reggie and he had a gun."

"Did you hear it go off?"

She shook her head. "I didn't. I didn't see or hear anything else until I came to as a prisoner of that deranged maniac who admitted he'd been in the room and had killed Quaid."

"I never cared for Lassiter," Bones said. "Arrogant. Always trying to act like he was an authority on stuff he knew nothing about."

Fielding shot him a look that even Jade recognized as a warning not to make those comments in front of Jade, Booker and Boros while the investigation was ongoing.

"I wouldn't try to tell you your business," Booker said, "but I've been running this around in my own mind ever since Jade first told me what happened. Just my two cents' worth, but I can't help wondering if Quaid might have initiated this crime himself and then it veered out of control."

"How do you mean?" Bones asked.

Booker explained his insurance-scam scenario.

"Interesting theory," Bones said. "If he trusted Lassiter to help him pull it off, looks like he made a deadly mistake."

"If all Vaquero wanted was someone to help him steal his own jewelry, why wouldn't he go with Javier?" Hampton asked. "They're supposed to be best friends from way back. You must have met him, Jade."

"He was Quaid's advance advocate. He's the one who hired Effacy and reserved the penthouse suite in this hotel," Jade explained. "Quaid was very close to him and his sister, Zoe. But Javier went back to Spain a few days after Quaid arrived in New York."

"That's not exactly accurate," Hampton said. "Javier left New York then, but he didn't leave the country. He was touring the West Coast with friends from Spain. He rushed back here as soon as he heard of Quaid's death."

"Then why did Zoe fly all the way over here to retrieve Quaid's body?" Jade asked.

"We need to table this discussion," Fielding said, his tone bordering on scolding. "Information about the investigation that doesn't concern Jade personally is confidential."

As usual, Fielding had taken control, but not before she'd found out that Javier was in New York. She was surprised Zoe hadn't mentioned that.

Fielding shook Booker's and Boros's hands and then turned to Jade. "Thanks for your input. I know this wasn't easy for you, but you've given us a few new details to consider. I'll get back to you and Boros tomorrow to schedule the lie-detector test. The three of you are free to go now."

"Good," Booker said. "Dinner calls."

"Can I give you a ride somewhere?" Boros offered. "I have a car waiting."

"To our hotel near Fifth and Central Park?"

"I can handle that."

Booker took Jade's arm as they followed Boros to the elevator.

"You did great," he said.

"Thanks. I'm sorry I ruined the evening you had planned."

"You're not getting off the hook that easily. You owe me a dance and the chance to do what Hampton and Bones have been dreaming about all night."

"See me fall off my shoes?"

"Not even close."

Chapter Sixteen

Jade was still wrestling with the outcome of the so-called reenactment when they reached the restaurant. If she was blacking out, why had Quaid's hands been at her throat? The only reason that made sense was to remove the necklace.

Had he been drugged or was he fully functioning? Fielding, Hampton and Bones all would have access to the toxicology report and knew the answer to that question. Yet one of them had asked her about his condition tonight.

Did they, like Zoe and Reggie, believe she had the necklace?

"I don't think I'll ever buy or wear another necklace in my life," she said as they followed the hostess past rows of tables still crowded with diners in spite of its being almost nine o'clock.

"Big convention in town," the hostess said. "Lots of requests for your reserved table, Mr. Knox, but the manager insisted we save it for you."

"I appreciate that."

The hostess pulled back a brocade curtain and held out a hand to usher them inside a private dining nook. Instead of chairs, a sofa for two provided the seating. A backdrop of soft music, a single rose on the table and candles to enhance the enchantment with their shimmery glow were waiting.

The anxiety that had plagued Jade's mind for days magically melted away.

"Your waiter will be with you momentarily, Mr. Knox." The hostess smiled a bit enviously at Jade. "Enjoy your evening."

"I'm blown away," Jade whispered once they were alone. "I can't believe you did all this. When did you do it?"

"I made a few calls while you were taking your marathon shower. Believe me, it was a sacrifice. I had to picture your beautiful body all wet and soapy without me there to help you get to those hard-to-reach places. But I figured a good steak was worth it."

"Make light all you want, Booker Knox. You can't deny that you're a romantic at heart."

"Actually, that's a newly discovered trait. But you should know that I can't take all the credit for this."

"What does that mean?"

"R.J. is worried sick about you."

"Sure he is. He's spent a lifetime worrying about me. What does he have to do with any of this?"

"He figures you've been through so much the last few days that you need and deserve a very special evening."

"So none of this is your idea?"

"The idea was all mine. The money is his. I decided this was the best we could do outside of breakfast at Tiffany's or midnight skinny-dipping in the French Riviera."

"Those would have been good options, too," she teased, determined not to let anything spoil this fairy-tale evening with Booker. R.J. had been right about one thing. She needed this night.

The waiter joined them, a bottle of red wine in hand.

"I took the liberty of ordering a Cabernet Sauvignon ahead of time," Booker said. "But if you'd rather have a cocktail first or a different wine, that's fine, too."

"No, your choice is great."

The waiter poured the wine and left a couple of menus.

"How hungry are you?" Booker asked as the waiter walked away.

"Not very," she admitted. "I'm still trying to push the images from my mind that I had to relive tonight."

He pushed the menus to the side. "Talk of murders and necklaces forbidden for the remainder of the evening."

"I like that idea. If I'm going to be treated like a princess, I should act like one."

"I daresay no princess ever looked as gorgeous as you do tonight, Your Majesty."

He leaned over and found her lips with his. The kiss was sweeter and a bit more restrained than the ones they'd shared earlier in the room. Still, her pulse quickened as erotic anticipation filled her senses.

"What shall we talk about?" she asked when the surge of desire eased enough that she was breathing normally again.

"Tell me about you."

"You already know about me. My mother moved to California with the dreamer who was to become number one when she was five months pregnant with me. My earliest memories are of them screaming at each other. They divorced the year I started kindergarten."

"I can see you now, bows in your curly hair, prissy, bossing everyone around and looking so adorable doing it you were still the teacher's pet."

"You read my biography. But in my defense, my mother insisted on the bows."

"What happened after kindergarten?"

"Number two came along. I liked him better. He didn't scream. He just went fishing and hunting. He even took me fishing with him on occasion. That's when I realized why he went fishing so often."

"Why is that?"

"My mother and her theatrics and dramatic mood changes were always lurking one misstep away."

"What happened to number two?"

"He lost his job and decided to move back to Montana. Mother had a bit part in a TV series by then, and her visions of becoming a star had reenergized. Their parting was fairly amiable."

"You seem to have your life divided into numbers."

"Mother changed according to who was the prominent man in her life, at least she did while the relationship was new. When I was in the sixth grade, Ben talked her into getting counseling."

"Ah, a name sneaked in there."

"Ben was my favorite. He was a hotel food manager and a wannabe chef. We ate really well while he was around, though I never learned to stomach foie gras or escargot. French names do not make goose liver or snails any more palatable to my way of thinking."

"Did your mother improve with counseling?"

"To some extent. I think mostly I learned to deal with her mood swings and over-the-top reactions. Like I said before, she is who she is, but she's Mom and I love her. Have to admit, though, we do get along better when there's a continent between us. And I do have her to thank or curse for my love of shopping and for shoes."

"And your good looks?"

"We favor. She's still attractive, though not the total knockout she was in her younger days. That was very daunting when I was a skinny, pimple-faced teenager."

"Not a pimple in sight tonight."

Booker snaked an arm around her shoulder. Her wine-glass was still half-full, but she was as giddy as if she'd drunk the whole bottle. She put her hand on his thigh, pressing gently, as the need for him swelled inside her.

The waiter took that moment to return, this time carrying a tray. He set an oyster dish in front of each of them. One look and she was suddenly famished.

"Our specialty of the house. Lightly grilled fresh oysters, drizzled with a mustard-crème sauce, sprinkled with minced bacon and delicate herbs. Compliments of the chef."

"Tell the chef thank-you and that I simply love oysters."

"Yes, ma'am. He'll be pleased. Would you care to order now?"

"Six more helpings of this," she joked.

"I'm sure that can be arranged."

Booker had picked up his menu and was scanning the choices.

"Why don't you order for both of us," she suggested.

"That could be risky."

"Oysters always put me in a risky mood."

"Six more orders," Booker seconded.

"We're only kidding," Jade assured the waiter.

Booker ordered a steak for two with salads and fully stuffed baked potatoes. Jade was certain it was far more than they could possibly eat.

This time when the waiter left, Booker forked an oyster and slipped it between her lips. The juices escaped and beaded in the corner of her mouth. Before she could wipe them away, Booker took care of it with a deliciously passionate kiss. By the time they finished the appetizer, the only thing she was hungry for was Booker.

"Care to dance?" he asked. "Seems a shame for our private dance floor to go to waste."

He took her hand and led her to their own small square of polished wood.

She knew that had been a mistake the second he took her into his arms. They swayed slowly, his body pressing into hers, heat flowing between them like embers ready to burst into flame.

"Were you in love with Quaid?"

The question stopped her cold. She pulled from his arms and looked him in the eye. "Where did that come from?"

"The way you talked about him in the hotel suite tonight. I'm not criticizing. I can see how you'd be seduced by him. Rich. Powerful. Talented. Sophisticated."

"Yes, he was all those things. I did find him attractive. For a moment I even wondered what it would be like to be courted by him and entertained on his fabulous yacht.

"But never for a second did he make me feel the way you do, Booker Knox. I've never wanted any man as much as I want you right now."

He kissed her and she marveled at how her life could be in such dangerous chaos and yet she never wanted this moment to end.

The waiter returned with their food.

"We'll take that to go," Booker said.

It was past midnight before they got around to the steaks. They ate every bite.

JADE SLAMMED HER empty coffee cup down on the bedside table. "That's it. I'm universally hated. I'm the abhorrent bitch who robbed the world of Quaid's creative genius."

He should have known when she turned on the TV, it was not the way to start the day. He stretched across her, picked up the remote from her bedside table and flicked it off. "The people making all the noise and accusations don't even know you."

"Maybe it's you who don't know me, Booker. Did you ever think of that?"

He tried to take her into his arms but she pulled away. "I'm serious."

"So am I," he asserted. "I know you intimately and I'm totally convinced of your innocence."

"Having sex with me makes you biased."

"Absolutely, but I believed you before we had mind-blowing sex. Kiki believes you."

"She's my mother. She has to believe me."

"I'm not sure that's an ironclad rule. But you also have John Boros and apparently all the Daltons in your corner. Once you take and pass the lie-detector test, I'm sure Detective Winston Fielding will be fully in your camp as well, if he's not already."

"I hope so. I had an uneasy feeling last night when I couldn't describe the men who were there with Reggie. I think I lost a little credibility."

"You were drugged at the time."

"And I assumed Quaid was, too, but now I'm not sure."

"Boros said your brother Travis is working on getting the toxicology report."

"When did you hear that?"

"Last night while the driver was helping you into the car as we left the hotel."

"Then I hope he's successful. Don't you find it strange that Travis is having anything to do with this?"

"No," Booker said. "I find it reasonable."

"I don't see how. We've never even met except for that hour or two at the original reading of R.J.'s will. He can't know that I'm innocent."

"I'm sure he's checked you out thoroughly and knows you have no criminal record. You don't, do you?"

"See, deep down you're not even sure."

"I wouldn't be serving you coffee in bed if I thought you were a killer or a thief. But back to Travis. Family aside, it makes perfect sense that he'd get involved in your case. He's a homicide detective the same as Fielding is and as Brit was. The good ones always seek justice and keep an open mind until all the facts are in."

"Too bad broadcasters and journalists don't have those same scruples."

Booker's phone vibrated. He picked it up. "It's your mother."

"Tell her I'm in the shower."

"She'll just call back."

Jade sighed. "Okay, hand me the phone."

Booker gave her the phone, then got out of bed and headed to the bathroom for a shower. In spite of the midnight-steak snack, he was getting hungry. Best to get breakfast while they could. Who knew when Fielding would call and expect them to rush over for the lie-detector test.

After that, with any luck, they could get out of New York and hopefully find someplace the paparazzi and Reggie Lassiter would not be able to track them down.

He poured a blob of shampoo into his hair and scrubbed vigorously while his mind went back to the crime scene and all the events that didn't quite add up.

By the time he was out of the shower and drying off, there was a tapping at the bathroom door.

"Booker."

He knotted the towel around his waist and opened the door. "Already miss me?"

"Yes, but that's not why I'm interrupting your shower."

"What's up?"

"Boros is on the phone. He called when I was trying to wind up the conversation with Mother."

"Is something wrong?"

"I'm not sure. He's set up a conference call with Leif and Travis and he wants both of us in on it. He wouldn't say more, just that it's imperative we talk."

Jade looked and sounded worried.

"It could be good news," Booker offered as he padded barefoot back to the bed, where she'd left his cell phone.

"Two attorneys and a homicide detective needing to talk to me and my bodyguard at the same time. The odds are not in my favor."

Even Booker couldn't come up with a denial for that.

"How are you holding up?" Leif asked when they joined the phone conference.

"I'm fine," Jade said, "unless you're calling with bad news."

"No, just new facts that Travis has come up with that I think might put a new slant on the investigation."

"Sorry I missed seeing both you and Booker when you were at the Dry Gulch," Travis chimed in. "I got back yesterday and plunged right into a backload of work, but I did take time to make a few phone calls on your behalf. I had a fax on my desk when I got back to it after working a double homicide for most of the night."

"Did you get any more on the toxicology report?" Booker asked.

"I did. Not sure why that hasn't been released, but Quaid did have a significant amount of Rohypnol and a smaller amount of Xanax in his system, which bears out Jade's story of the champagne being drugged."

"Did you get any information on the dead man who delivered the champagne to the hotel suite?" Boros asked.

"Yes. His name is Arnold Rowling. Long rap sheet that includes writing hot checks, burglarizing homes and selling drugs to minors. He got out of jail three months ago after serving time for causing significant injuries to a female clerk during a strong-arm robbery of a convenience store. Reggie Lassiter was the arresting officer in that case."

"So he knew Rowling was without scruples," Jade said.

"No doubt about that," Travis agreed. "Also interesting is that Rowling dated a woman named Miriam Law who worked in the hotel where Quaid was murdered before he did time. She no longer works there and claims she hasn't seen Rowling since he got out of prison."

"If she didn't claim it under oath, it doesn't mean a thing," Boros said. "She might not even tell the truth when she is under oath."

"What about the hotel's surveillance cameras?" Booker asked. "It seems they would have picked up anyone entering or leaving one of the penthouse suites, especially someone carrying Jade when she was passed out cold."

"The cameras would have picked that up, had someone not blocked them out."

"I'm guessing a law enforcement officer like Reggie could easily do that."

"Right, but he missed one camera," Travis said. "The one that showed him pushing a laundry cart apparently filled with dirty towels from the service elevator to a back exit used mostly by employees going to take a smoke or smuggle goods out of the building. Management had that one well hidden."

"He stuffed me in a cart and covered me with wet towels."

"That doesn't rank up there with being kidnapped and shot at," Travis reminded her.

"It makes my blood boil, anyway."

"That's it for what I have," Travis said. "I'm not sure how helpful it is, but I wanted to pass it along."

"Everything helps," Boros said.

"Good. I'll keep digging up what I can. But if Detective Fielding says you can leave the state after you take the lie-detector test, Jade, I have a suggestion with a generous offer attached for you and Booker."

"Let's hear it," Booker said.

"We have a neighbor with a corporate jet who's offered to send it to New York to pick you two up and bring you back to the Dry Gulch whenever the NYPD says you can leave the city. That way you won't be subjected to risks from Lassiter or the accusing glares of other passengers on a commercial flight."

"Most of whom have already decided I'm guilty of murder," Jade said. "Why is this neighbor of yours any different?"

"Maybe they believe in innocent until proven guilty. At any rate, it's the Lambert family. They own the Bent Pine Ranch and Lambert, Incorporated."

"I'd take them up on that offer in a New York minute," Booker said, "but that decision has to be up to Jade."

"I'll give it some thought," she said, "but first I have to make it through the lie-detector test. Screw that up and Fielding may decide he's taken enough heat and toss me to the wolves."

They talked a few more minutes, mostly small talk and repeats of what had gotten them to this point. Booker's mind had moved on to exactly how he was going to keep Jade safe in a city that not only never slept but never slowed down.

Chapter Seventeen

"You have a lot of nerve showing up in public."

"Murderer. Murderer. Murderer."

The strange woman had stuck her face between Jade and Booker and waved a finger in Jade's face while her chant grew louder and louder. Before Jade could escape, two more women had left their tables and their uneaten breakfasts to join in the condemning mantra.

Booker shoved his chair back and stood, positioning himself between Jade and the hovering women. "That's enough. Stand back *now*."

The authority in his voice and his imposing stance got their attention long enough for Jade to stand. By that time, a manager and two waiters had rushed over to help diffuse the situation.

Tears burned in the corners of Jade's eyes. She had never felt so hated before.

Booker rushed her out of the hotel's café and to the nearest elevator with a guiding hand to the small of her back.

"It's not fair. I'm the victim. Why can't they see that?"

"They're like parrots, mimicking what they hear on TV and read in the papers and on the internet. When the full truth comes out, they'll all be shouting for justice for you."

"I'd love to believe you, Booker Knox, but we both know you're just saying what you think I want to hear."

They went back to the room and she kicked out of her shoes and threw herself across the bed. She beat her fist into the pillow a few times and then rolled over and faced him.

"Call Leif, please. Tell him I'm ready to fly to the Dry Gulch Ranch the second Detective Fielding okays it. I know I can't hide out there forever, but I've had enough of this."

"And more than you should have to take."

"I came within a heartbeat of stuffing my whole biscuit into that woman's big mouth. Just imagine the kind of field day the reporters could have had with that."

"Your mother would have had my phone ringing for hours."

"With great advice for me like I should never order biscuits. They'll ruin my figure."

"I'm with your mother on that one. Don't go ruining that figure."

"Ha-ha. That's the other thing. People shouldn't have to ring you to talk to me. I'm getting a phone as soon as we get to Dallas even if I have to buy one of those throwaways."

"You certainly can't have a listed number. Crackpots would never give you a moment's peace."

"The way I never give you a moment's peace. You can't even enjoy your breakfast without being attacked by women chanters. You have to be fed up with being my babysitter."

"I'm your bodyguard, not your babysitter. There's a difference."

"Right. Bodyguards carry guns and get shot at."

"And get to save the beautiful damsel in distress." He walked over and lay down beside her.

She'd love to roll over and slide into his arms, but that would only be a heavenly reprieve to lull her into believing this would all work out. No wonder Booker couldn't wait to get back to the Dry Gulch Ranch. He would probably catch the first flight to California as soon as he'd dropped her into the hands of her family.

If he did, that really would be the final straw.

She'd never fallen for any man the way she'd fallen for Booker, never dreamed it possible. He seemed just as crazy about her, but he'd never even hinted at a future together beyond his leave.

She couldn't fault him for that. She might not even have a future. So why was she wasting the time they did have together with her useless rant?

Booker was here and so was she. Rolling into his arms, she lifted her lips to his. Those women in the café could have their anger.

Jade had Booker—at least for now.

BOOKER WAS STARING out the hotel window overlooking Central Park wondering when the next hit would come, when his cell phone vibrated. He grabbed it from the edge of the desk and checked the caller ID.

Zoe Aranda. He hesitated to answer. Jade didn't need another upsetting encounter today.

Jade stared at him questioningly.

"It's Zoe again," he said. "We can ignore the call."

She made a disgruntled face. "It can't be worse than women chanting 'murderer' like irate, middle-aged cheerleaders." She reached out her hand for the phone.

Reluctantly, he handed it over. A few seconds later, the

look on her face and the tone of her voice indicated Jade had been wrong. There was a good chance this was worse.

"JADE, THIS IS JAVIER, Quaid's friend."

"And Zoe's brother. I remember you."

"Hopefully kindly. I must ask a favor."

He sounded anxious. "What kind of favor?"

"It's my sister, Zoe. I don't know how to help her."

"Is she ill?"

"She's not herself. I've never seen her so upset."

"Did something happen?"

"She'd just been sitting in one of the kitchen chairs all morning and staring at nothing. Then she started crying. Not a few tears, like she's been doing since Quaid's death. Sobs. She won't stop. I've tried everything, but she won't stop."

"Hand her the phone. Perhaps she'll tell me why she's so upset."

"Hold on."

Javier was back in less than a minute. "She won't talk. She just cries and says she's going to kill herself."

"Is this about Quaid's death?"

"I think yes. And about that damn missing necklace."

The one Zoe thought Jade had stolen. "What about the necklace?"

"She thinks it's cursed and that somehow she caused that. I try to tell her there is no curse, but she won't believe me. Please, Jade. Come and see if she will listen to you."

"I'm not sure I'm the best person to do that."

"She trusts you. You were Quaid's friend. If she won't listen to you, what hope is there?"

When he put it that way, what else could she do but go and give it a shot? "Where are you?" Jade asked.

"In a friend's apartment. He's letting me use it while he's working out of town. Zoe is staying with me until they release Quaid's body."

"Where is this apartment?"

"In the lower city."

"Lower Manhattan?"

"Yes. That is it."

"Give me the address."

Jade scribbled the information down using the pen and pad of paper furnished by the hotel. "I'll be there as soon as I can. Don't leave Zoe alone."

"No, I will be with my poor sister. I think her heart is breaking."

"Where is it we're going?" Booker asked when she broke the connection.

"That was Zoe's brother, Javier. Apparently, Zoe is having a meltdown and threatening suicide. I think I'm the only person she knows in New York. I have to try to help."

"How much do you really know about Zoe or her brother?"

"I know that Zoe is upset and in desperate need of a friend. I can't just ignore a call for help."

Booker picked up his keys. "For the record, I'm not comfortable with this."

"There's nothing to worry about. I'll just talk to her. If I think she's suicidal, I'll call the police."

"I'm holding you to that."

THE TAXI STOPPED in front of an old apartment building in a seedy area. Impulsively, Booker touched his pistol that was conveniently resting in his shoulder holster. But that wasn't the only weapon he was carrying today.

The knife that he'd wielded so expertly on past SEAL

missions was also on ready and holstered inside his boot. He didn't expect to have to use either, but he wouldn't hesitate if it was necessary to save Jade's life.

They stepped inside the building. Graffiti covered the walls, much of it lewd. A steep staircase was located to the left of the narrow hallway. There was no elevator.

A perfect place to lay a trap.

Alarms echoed through Booker's mind. He stopped and pulled Jade against the wall. "I'm calling for backup."

"It's Zoe we're talking about, Booker. She's not going to shoot us."

"When in doubt, always trust your instincts." That little gem had saved his life more than once.

He punched in Fielding's cell-phone number. Thankfully, the detective answered. Booker explained the situation. "I'm probably overreacting, but something about this call for help doesn't feel right."

"You were wise to call," Fielding said. "I'd much rather send backup than an ambulance."

Ten minutes later, four officers in street clothes arrived as promised. They, Booker and Jade stepped back outside and into the bright light of day to go over the plan.

They'd keep it simple. Booker and Jade would go inside and talk to Zoe and Javier. The officers would be two doors down, acting as if they were just chatting or comparing notes.

If Booker needed them, he was to start talking extremely loud. Help would be seconds away.

Booker's senses were on keen alert as he tapped on the door to Javier's apartment.

Javier answered the door. "What do you want?"

Jade pushed in front of Booker. "Booker's a friend of mine."

Javier glared at Booker and then turned to Jade. "I

was expecting you to come alone." He shrugged. "But it doesn't matter, as long as you came."

Booker scanned the disgustingly dirty and extremely cluttered apartment. It wasn't until his gaze reached the farthest corner of the room that he realized the terrifying truth.

His hunch had been right again.

Chapter Eighteen

Zoe was gagged and tied to a chair, terror etched into every line of her face. Reggie Lassiter stood next to her with a .45 pointed at her head. Javier dropped to a chair and buried his head in his hands.

"One wrong move and Zoe's dead," Reggie warned. "The second bullet is for Jade."

Shudders shook Zoe's body as if they were in the middle of an earthquake.

"I'm so sorry, Jade," Javier said. "I didn't want to call you. I had no choice. If I didn't follow Reggie Lassiter's orders, he would kill my dear, sweet sister." Anxiety chipped at his words.

Reggie grinned as if this were all some harmless joke. "You had your chances to play nice, Jade. All you had to do was give me the necklace and I would be soaking up the sun on some little paradise island. But you just wouldn't listen to reason."

"So you're the one who sent Zoe to me yesterday," Jade said.

Her voice was hard as nails. As soft as she was when she was in Booker's arms, she was as tough as they came when the going got rough. But she was no match for Reggie and a pistol. Booker had sworn to protect her. He had to find a way to get her out of this alive.

The police were waiting just outside. If Booker called to them they could be there in seconds. But it would only take one second for Reggie to pull the trigger.

"Both of you, back up against the wall," Reggie ordered. "Booker, put your hands in the air. Javier, take his pistol from his shoulder holster."

Javier crossed the floor slowly, took Booker's gun and scooted it across the floor to Reggie.

"So, what do you plan to do, Reggie?" Jade asked. "Kill all of us the way you killed Vaquero and Rowling?"

"You have this all wrong. I'm just a man trying to get my cut of the pie. That's why I'm going to give you one last chance, Jade. Tell me where you've hidden the necklace and this can all be over without anyone firing a shot."

"Release Zoe and I'll take you to the necklace."

Reggie chuckled. "It seems to me I've fallen for that one before. I have a better idea. You tell Javier where it is, a little secret the two of you can share. I'll give him two hours to get back here with it. One minute past that and Zoe's brains will add a new level of gore to the apartment's decor."

"That hardly seems fair," Booker said. "After all, Jade did outsmart you. She deserves something for that. We'll tell you where the necklace is if you'll split the money you make from it with us."

Reggie laughed. "Why take half when I can have it all?"

Zoe had stopped crying, but her eyes were so swollen, Booker didn't fathom how she could see out of them.

Javier's expression remained the same as it had been ever since they'd walked in. Stern. Resolute. Helpless. Maybe all of the above, but his expression was impossible to read.

"What do you say, Booker?" Jade asked.

Reggie inched the gun closer so that the barrel pushed into Zoe's skin.

Javier yelled at Reggie to stop tormenting her. A yell. The signal the cops were waiting on. The door flew open. Booker went for the knife.

Reggie changed his aim. The knife was already flying through the air headed straight for Reggie's heart.

The blade hit its mark, but Reggie didn't go down instantly. He managed to stay on his feet the split second it took to pull the trigger. The bullet missed Jade by inches, burrowing into the wall behind her head.

Javier looked as if he was sliding into shock. Finally he reached behind Zoe's back and untied her. She yanked the gag from her mouth.

Reggie fell to the floor in a pool of his own blood.

Zoe gathered Javier into her arms, her tears soaking the front of his shirt.

Jade's eyes filled with tears, as well.

Booker pulled back, his insides quaking at how close he'd come to losing Jade.

"He would have killed me," Zoe whispered.

"From the trajectory of that bullet, I'd say Jade Dalton is the one he really wanted to kill," one of the officers said.

Another officer knelt and checked Reggie's pulse. "Looks like you not only saved lives and reeled in Reggie Lassiter for us, Mr. Knox, but you just saved the city the price of a costly trial."

"He's dead?" Zoe questioned as if she couldn't believe it.

"He's dead."

"Justice," she murmured. "Thank God. He admitted he killed my beloved friend, Quaid Vaquero."

Booker and Jade were forced to hang around and answer questions until Fielding arrived almost an hour later. After he'd heard the details, Fielding complimented Booker on a job well done. Quaid's killer was dead. Jade was free to go on with her life.

"If I ever need a bodyguard again, I'm finding me a Navy SEAL on leave," Jade said as they descended the staircase. "I thought you were overreacting when you called for backup. How did you know we were walking into a trap?"

"Experience, training and a lucky hunch."

"Any other hunches?"

"I have a hunch this is going to be a great afternoon."

"I have a hunch you're right. Thanks for saving my life."

"All in a day's work." A day that had surely taken ten years from his life.

"With Reggie dead, you can go back to your vacation that I so rudely interrupted," Jade said. "You have enough leave left to spend a couple of weeks on the Dry Gulch playing cowboy, bonding with Kimmie and getting to know Brit."

Booker stopped walking. "There you go again. I'm starting to feel like you don't like having me around."

"Definitely not true. I just thought—"

"No more thoughts like that," he interrupted before she wrote him right out of her life. "Spending the rest of my leave at the Dry Gulch sounds great to me—as long as you're there. But I'm not planning on going anywhere without you."

"In that case, cowboy, saddle up and let's join the family roundup at the Dry Gulch Ranch."

"Are you sure?" he asked.

"Yes. I've faced a killer. Surely I can face R.J. and a heaping hassle of family."

Booker took out his phone and made a flight reservation before she could change her mind.

THE UNITED AIRLINES flight landed in Dallas at three the following afternoon. The Lamberts' offer of a private jet still stood, but Jade deemed it unnecessary now that she had been the much-maligned heroine who'd helped capture Quaid's killer instead of being a murder suspect.

It was amazing how quickly a nation's fickle opinions could shift. Speculation about the missing necklace continued, but even that barely got a mention in the morning news.

A few passengers had stared when she passed them in the aisle while boarding the plane. None spoke. With the danger past, Jade had time to think about Quaid as the nice, talented person he was and mourn his death more appropriately.

For Zoe and Javier the grief surely went much deeper. They'd lost a lifelong friend who'd stayed close even as he rose to fame and wealth. Zoe had worked side by side with him for all her adult life. In the end, that devotion to Quaid had almost cost both Zoe and Javier their lives.

Booker stopped to wait on Jade as she fell behind in the crowded airport. "Not already having regrets about coming back to Texas, are you?"

"Not yet." That would come later. "I'm just having a melancholy moment about all that's happened over the past few days."

"That's normal. Postbattle syndrome. Replays of what went wrong and what went right. Do you want to stop, grab a beer and regroup?"

"No. I'm ready to move on." Her time with Booker would be over too soon, as it was. She couldn't afford to waste a second of it on things she could do nothing about.

She hurried alongside Booker as they made their way to the car-rental booth. Booker got in line and then scanned the area.

"Are you expecting someone to meet us?" Jade asked.

"Not sure. Last time I was here, this gorgeous auburn-haired babe rushed up and kissed me senseless. I was hoping for a repeat."

"Is that right?"

"Yeah. If she shows up again, you don't mind if we give her a ride, do you?"

"What kind of ride?"

"Any kind she wants."

"She'd have to be a fool to turn down an offer like that." Jade was nobody's fool. She threw her arms around Booker's neck and kissed him hungrily. "To be continued," she said when she pulled away, still breathless from the passion soaring inside her.

Once they were in the rental, Booker found some country music and they both joined in a song with George Strait.

"You have a good voice," Jade said.

"I played the guitar and was the lead singer in a band once."

"Really? You are full of surprises, Booker Knox."

"Before you get too impressed, I was in the eighth grade and the band practiced in the drummer's garage. We called ourselves the Howlers. That was a fairly accurate description of our talent, but we played a couple of gigs for tips at the local ice-cream shop. One night we actually made enough to buy banana splits."

"Wow. Big-time. What happened to the band?"

"The drummer failed algebra. His parents kicked us out of the garage and made him spend his afternoons studying."

"Bummer. That covers your musical talents. Moving on, did you actually know anything about ranching or do you just like the idea of being a cowboy?"

"I'll have you know, I worked my tail off pitching hay and branding steers on by grandpa's ranch up in Oklahoma. I've even roped steers and I'm a whiz at rope tricks."

"So you're not actually an imitation cowboy."

"I'm the real deal."

In a lot more ways than one. That, she knew for certain.

A few minutes later, Booker swerved into the exit lane and then turned right at the first traffic light and into the parking lot of a strip-shopping center.

She was about to ask why, when she saw the huge sign for a Western-clothing store. "Do you need a new Stetson or is it boots you're after, cowboy?"

"Both, but not for me. As good as you look in those nosebleed heels, they are not going to cut it in the horse barn."

"Another of R.J.'s ideas?"

"Nope, this one's on me."

By the time they left the store, she was wearing a pair of Wranglers, a teal Western shirt with pearl buttons, a pair of goat-roper boots and a white Stetson angled to give the outfit attitude.

There were more jeans and shirts in a giant shopping bag, most items that Booker had chosen for her. He'd insisted on picking up the tab for everything.

Not only was there no arguing with him when he was in the SEAL protective mode, but there was also no arguing with cowboy Booker, either. If they were to see each other after his leave was up, there would definitely be some power struggles between them in the days to come.

And some makeup sessions that would make the earth fly off its orbit.

By the time they reached the Dry Gulch, Jade had psyched herself up to deal with R.J. When they opened the front door, and every one of the resident Daltons and a few faces she didn't recognize greeted her with a chorus of "Welcome home," her determination turned to a whirlwind of mixed emotions.

It was like diving into a pool of roses. It looked beautiful and inviting, but there had to be thorns hidden in there somewhere.

No THORNS APPEARED at dinner. Only food and lots of it, all delicious. Sliced brisket, roast chicken, potato salad, fresh field peas cooked with big hunks of ham, summer squash stewed in tomatoes and onions, homemade rolls, chocolate cake and coconut-cream pies, all washed down with pitchers of iced tea and topped off with decaffeinated coffee.

Then the women had been pushed from the kitchen to gather on the front porch while the men nursed beers and promised to take care of the cleanup chores.

It was Jade's first meeting with Travis's wife, Faith. She was impressed immediately. Faith was not only attractive and self-confident, she was funny and delightful to be around. And Carolina Lambert, the neighbor who'd come for the celebration, was absolutely beautiful and far more down-to-earth than Jade would have expected from someone so wealthy.

Jade settled in the porch swing hoping they weren't

going to bombard her with questions about the ordeal with Reggie and the Arandas.

To head them off, Jade started the conversation, steering it in another direction. "If I keep eating like this, I won't be able to snap these new jeans."

"If you need exercise, you can always borrow Lila and Lacy," Hadley offered, nodding toward her four-year-old twin daughters who were giggling and chasing fireflies. "Keeping up with them will melt the pounds away."

"So that's how you keep that great figure," Carolina Lambert said. "And here I thought Adam had you out chopping wood."

"No, that's how he keeps his great body," Hadley teased.

"I hope I get my figure back once the baby's born," Leif's wife, Joni, said, patting her belly. "But I'm glad there's only one on the way to our household. I am not the ball of energy Hadley is."

"You are much too modest, Joni. If I worked the hours you do, taking care of every horse in the county, I'd come straight home and collapse every night."

"Who says I don't?"

"Speaking of horses, Jade, you and Booker should ride down to Shadow Junction one day soon," Faith suggested.

Her name linked with Booker's. Jade liked that a lot. "What's Shadow Junction?"

"It's where two rivers meet on the far northwest corner of the ranch. It's on the edge of a piney forest. In late afternoon, the deep shadows make the area seem at least ten degrees cooler than it really is."

"It's a favorite watering hole of deer, too," Hadley said, "but the men like it because fishing is good there."

Joni stretched and shifted positions in the porch rocker, no doubt trying to get comfortable. "There's an old, one-room log cabin out there," Joni said, "rather dilapidated, but interesting. Some locals claim it used to be the schoolhouse, but R.J. says it was the foreman's cabin back when he was a kid. It's tucked so deep into the woods you don't know it's there until you practically stumble into it."

"Lila started crying and leaped into Adam's arms the first time she saw it," Hadley said. "It took us a while to convince her that it wasn't the cabin where the witch from 'Hansel and Gretel' lived."

"I tend to agree with Lila on that one," Faith said. "I suggested tearing it down, but Travis thinks the guys should fix it up and turn it into a fish-cleaning spot and shelter for days they get caught in a rainstorm while fishing."

"Booker and I will definitely check it out," Jade said.

"I'm really glad you came back," Carolina said. "I can't tell you how much it means to R.J. He was so afraid for you, I thought he might wind up in the hospital."

Jade grew instantly uneasy. She wasn't sure why, but any inference about how R.J. felt about her seemed to fill her with guilt.

Thankfully, Brit, who'd arrived late to the conversation because of putting Kimmie to bed, changed the subject. Nonetheless, Jade was glad when the men joined them and soon after, they all went their separate ways.

Thorns had a way of festering long after the delicate petals fell away. R.J. had become her thorn.

ZOE CLOSED HER eyes and rested her head on the back of the seat as the plane took off for the long flight back to Barcelona.

The only man she'd ever loved was dead. She'd planned to grow old with Quaid, imagined nights by the fire and summers in the sun. One day he would have grown weary of the models, starlets and sparkling young beauties like Jade Dalton.

He would have realized that Zoe was his true love. That had been her dream since she was the skinny, annoying kid chasing after Quaid and her big brother.

Now she'd lost them both. Quaid to a bullet and Javier to a dark side she didn't understand.

He was staying in America. She was going home to an empty life and a broken heart.

Her biggest regret was designing the necklace, a masterpiece that was supposed to make Quaid love her. Instead, it had led to his death.

The tragic irony of that would haunt her for the rest of her life.

Chapter Nineteen

The smell of horseflesh, the wind in his face, a magnificent mount and Jade Dalton riding at his side. Life couldn't get much better than this. Unless he started to think about the fact that it was almost over.

"That must be Shadow Junction up ahead," Jade said. "I'm not sure I'd call those rivers, but there are definitely two bodies of swiftly moving water merging at the edge of that thick stretch of pine trees."

"Exactly where R.J. said it would be. That man knows his spread down to every lightning-bent tree, body of water, clump of bull nettle and dogwood tree. Probably knows half his cattle by name."

"That's surely stretching things," Jade said, "but as long as you can follow the directions back to the house when we leave, I'll be satisfied."

"Getting lost in the woods could have its perks," Booker teased.

"Yes, but those might include poison ivy, mosquitoes and vicious wasps."

"Not to mention snakes," Booker added.

"So why did you?"

Booker dismounted and then offered his assistance to Jade. They walked their horses to the water for a drink.

"The towering pine trees do cast long shadows," Jade said. "In places, the rivers almost look black."

"Looks like a great place to teach you to fish," Booker said.

"What makes you think I don't already know how?"

"Do you?"

"No. Number two wanted to teach me, but Mother was afraid he'd let me drown."

"Speaking of your mother, have you talked to her since we left New York?"

"I did. She's back to her old self now that I'm safe, fretting about the new wrinkles worrying about me caused. It was probably a mistake mentioning we were at the Dry Gulch, though. She's just liable to fly down for a reunion."

Booker laughed. "That might shake things up a bit." He secured their horses and, hand in hand, they followed a path into the woods.

"I'm not sure I like this place," Jade said. "It gives me the chills."

Booker let go of her hand and slipped an arm around her waist. "We can go back if you want."

"No. I have to at least see the witch's cabin."

"No witches around here. The spiders and stinging scorpions killed them all before Davy Crockett arrived."

"You are not making this any easier."

Yet Jade appeared to relax as she related the rest of what she'd heard about this place last night.

When they finally reached the cabin, Booker figured dilapidated was much too generous a description. "Let's go inside," Jade said.

"I wouldn't advise it."

"Just for a peek."

Booker stepped onto a pile of rocks that someone had used to replace the rotted steps. The rest of the structure looked reasonably sound, considering that the chimney had collapsed. There was no glass left in the windows and dirt dobbers and wasp nests served as decoration for the log walls.

Jade took one step inside, then screamed.

A second later, Booker spied the culprit. A giant, hairy Texas brown tarantula was reacting to being disturbed. It was kicking toward the door, its front legs raised as if it was ready to attack.

Booker had to work to hide a smile as he stepped outside with Jade. "You weren't that afraid when Reggie pointed a gun at you."

"Reggie didn't have eight hairy legs."

"Point made. Guess that means you don't want to make out in the log cabin."

"Excellent guess."

"Then we should head back to the house. I'm about a minute away from kissing you and starting something I won't be able to stop."

A heartbeat later she was in his arms. They made love on a thick carpet of pine straw. Shadow Junction rose to perfection as the sun began its drop to the horizon. Never had cool been so hot.

A WEEK INTO their stay at Dry Gulch Ranch, Jade had to admit that she had never been happier in all her life. She gave full credit for that to Booker. He kept life exciting and fun. They never talked of the future, though it loomed in front of them constantly.

His love of ranch life and wide-open spaces had even begun to rub off on her. They'd been horseback riding, taken long walks, gone four-wheeling down the dry gulch the ranch had been named for and she'd even learned to fix a broken strand of barbed-wire fence.

Most surprising was that the huge Dalton clan she'd expected to be overwhelming wasn't. Today Booker and Jade were babysitting Kimmie while Brit had gone to Dallas with Joni for her seven-month checkup.

Watching her tough SEAL with the cowboy roots interact with Kimmie tugged at Jade's every heartstring. Right now he was lying on the floor with her on his stomach. His antics kept the adorable baby laughing.

"You'd make a great father, Booker Knox."

"Maybe one day, but definitely not while I'm still a SEAL. A father needs to be home a lot more often than I'd be."

"Surely some SEALs are married, with babies."

"Yep."

Yep. That was it. No explanation or further justification. It shouldn't get to her, but it did. It wasn't as if Booker had ever promised anything more than spending time together while he was on leave. If he had, it would have scared her off. She'd gone into this affair with her eyes wide-open, neither expecting nor seeking any form of commitment.

She'd never counted on falling in love. R.J. walked in from the kitchen carrying a toolbox.

"Do you need some help?" Booker asked.

"You look like you already have your hands full. I'm just putting the repaired cap back on the newel post at the second-floor landing."

"I noticed it was missing," Jade said. "How did it get broken?"

"It wasn't actually broken. It just needed some sanding and refinishing. Lila laid a slightly used lollipop there one day and the candy stuck to it so bad Mattie Mae had to take a knife to it to scrape it off."

"I take it the post got a little scratched up in the process," Booker said. He handed Kimmie off to Jade and followed R.J. up the stairs.

"I'm not much with woodworking," Booker said. "I'll just watch and see how a master does it."

"Adam did most of the fixin'. He sanded it down on the lathe," R.J. said. "There was a time I could fix anything that broke around here. Now I'm doing good to climb the steps without tripping."

Jade carried Kimmie up the stairs to watch the repair job. What R.J. had referred to as the cap was actually a beautiful finial, much like the one that had been on the spindle-like posts that supported the mirror in Quaid's hotel suite.

"The finial seemed to screw on fairly easily," Jade said.

"More child's play than man's work," R.J. admitted.

"Are the posts always solid?"

"Depends on their purpose. This one's solid. Many times they're hollow."

"And if they were hollow, someone could unscrew the finial, drop something inside and then screw the top back on in a matter of seconds."

"Something like a two-hundred-and-twenty-five-million-dollar necklace?" Booker asked.

"You are in mental tune with me."

"I am if you're thinking that we may have just solved the case of the missing necklace."

"Hell's bells!" R.J. bellowed. "Now, wouldn't that be something? I might have just helped solve a mystery."

"Don't count it solved yet," Booker said. "The CSU may already have checked there, but it's sure worth a call to Detective Fielding."

Kimmie started to fuss. Jade held her tight and sang to her as they all went downstairs to make the call.

"If we do find the necklace, I hope Quaid left it to Zoe," Jade said as Booker punched in the number. "She's worked with him for so long and was thoroughly devoted. I think she might even have been in love with him."

It was two hours later before they got a call back from Detective Fielding. Booker handed Jade the phone so she could get the news first.

"Are you sitting down?" Fielding asked.

"You found the necklace."

"Right where you said to look."

Jade squealed her pleasure and Booker put an arm around her shoulders to share in the excitement.

"I think we can put a lid on this case now," Fielding said. "Quaid must have figured the drugged champagne meant trouble. He hid the necklace and then dragged the mirror back into the bedroom so it would hopefully go unnoticed. Reggie Lassiter never had a clue."

"I just wish it had saved Quaid's life," she said.

"Unfortunately, it didn't work out that way. I'm really sorry for all the trouble and danger this cost you, Jade. But it's over now. You can come home and put your life back in order."

Home. As if anyplace without Booker would ever feel like home again. Even the excitement of big-city life had lost its appeal unless Booker was there, too.

"I'm sure Booker has a few questions," Jade said. "I'll pass the phone to him."

"I have one favor of you two," Fielding said. "I'd like you to keep this quiet for at least in the family. I'm sure the mayor will want to deliver the news in a press conference."

"No problem."

The case was closed. And in another week, her life with Booker would be, too.

Unless she took matters into her own hands. After all, Booker wasn't the only one with skills. She had her own talents and the wardrobe to enhance them.

BOOKER HAD JUST turned off the light and spooned himself around Jade's sleeping body when his phone rang. He grabbed it and took it into the hall so as not to wake her.

"I hope I didn't catch you at a bad time."

"I wasn't asleep, but I was in bed." He tried to place the voice but couldn't. "Who is this?"

"Javier Aranda."

Booker wasn't expecting that. "Are you back in Spain?"

"No, actually, I'm on my way to Dallas, Texas, not far from where you are staying. I should get there sometime tomorrow afternoon."

"What brings you down here?"

"Just touring. I decided to spend some more time in your country while I was here. Airfare is very costly. Once I return to Spain, I may never make it back to America again."

"Is your sister with you?"

"She is not. I tried to talk Zoe into staying, but she was still too upset over Quaid's death to enjoy sightseeing."

Obviously Javier wasn't. "How did you find out Jade and I are in Texas?"

"I was able to reach Jade's mother in California. She was most helpful."

Good old Mom. Booker wasn't keen on the idea of Javier visiting Jade. She was doing a terrific job of putting the murders behind her. She didn't need a reminder of the nightmare.

"Do you think I could drive out to Oak Grove and meet the two of you for lunch one day later in the week?"

"I don't think we can make that, Javier. We have a lot going on. I have your number. If things change, I'll call you."

"I sure hope we can work something out," Javier said. "Zoe had made a jeweled memento to thank Jade. She'd really like Jade to have it."

"Perhaps you can mail it to her. I assume you have the address."

"Yes, I do."

"Enjoy your travels, Javier."

"I will. Enjoy your life, Booker Knox."

Javier was clearly not happy with being turned down, but there was something more about him that didn't sit right with Booker. It wasn't a full-blown hunch, but Booker had an idea that Javier had been taking advantage of his friendship with Quaid for years. Trips to America. Living the good life. One of the hangers-on bunch that always hook onto the wealthy.

Not that any of that really mattered now.

JADE WOKE TO an almost blinding glare. The sun was already high enough in the spring sky to shine directly into the bedroom. She rolled over and reached for Booker. His side of the bed was empty, the sheet tossed back.

She checked the time as she threw her legs over the side of the bed. Almost nine o'clock. Central time. She hadn't slept this late in years.

In minutes, her teeth were brushed and she was dressed in jeans and a pale yellow shirt she'd picked up at an Oak Grove boutique yesterday.

Not wanting to waste time on her hair, she ran a brush through it and pulled it back into a ponytail. One of the advantages of not having to rush into a New York corporate office every day.

Stopping at the head of the stairs, she took another look at the newly refinished finial. Timing was everything. If R.J. had replaced it a week sooner or two weeks later, or if Lila had not used it as a candy dish, Quaid's beautiful work of jeweled art might have been lost for all time.

R.J. had a new claim to fame. R.J., the dad who had never been part of her life. Leaving him might have been the best decision her mother had ever made.

Numbers one through five had their problems, but none had dealt with the crippling addictions that R.J. admitted had claimed most of his life. Were it not for the brain tumor he might still be battling the demons.

Jade doubted she'd ever think of him as a father. He hadn't been in any real sense of the word. Still, she was glad she'd had this chance to meet him. He had a warmth to him she'd never expected. Given time, she might even share a closeness with him. Her experiences on the Dry Gulch Ranch had definitely given the concept of family a whole new meaning.

She was a Dalton and it was growing on her.

And Booker liked R.J. That counted for a lot.

She was halfway down the stairs before she heard voices drifting from the kitchen. Brit's. Hadley's. R.J.'s. But not Booker's.

"You look right chipper this morning," R.J. said as she joined them.

"Well rested," she said. "I can't believe I slept this late." They were all sitting around the kitchen table, but the breakfast dishes had been cleared away and their coffee mugs were all empty.

"Relief from tension," Brit said, shifting a wiggly Kimmie from one side of her lap to the other. "Knowing the missing necklace is now in the hands of the NYPD must have given you some much-needed closure."

"I suppose that's it." She filled herself a mug of coffee and took it back to the table with her. "Does anyone know where Booker is?"

Kimmie slapped her chubby little hands on the table and looked around as if she was expecting him.

"He, Cannon and Adam took the ATVs up to our place," Hadley said as she pushed back from the table. "I love the company and the coffee was great, but I want to exercise a couple of horses before it's time to pick up Lila and Lacy from preschool."

She carried her mug to the sink. "How about going with me, Jade? It's a beautiful morning for riding. We can go to Shadow Junction. I planted some agapanthus bulbs near there last fall and I want to see if the deer ate them or let them grow."

"Sounds great as long as I don't have to go inside the log cabin. I intruded on a very large and hairy tarantula when I went there with Booker. I suspect he's just lying in wait for my return."

Brit laughed. "And probably invited a few cousins to the welcoming party. I stay clear of that place myself."

"You can finish your coffee on the way to the horse barn," Hadley said. "If you're hungry, grab a hunk of banana bread. That will keep you from starving until we get back."

Jade refilled her mug with coffee but let the sweet treat ride. One step outside the back door and she felt a wave of anxiety that made no sense. The sky was a cloudless cover of blue. A slight breeze carried the scent of pine, clover and spring blooms. The dew looked like diamonds scattered at their feet.

What could possibly go wrong?

JAVIER PULLED UP in front of the ranch house. An old man sat on the front porch. Other than that, there was no one in sight. This might be easier than he had expected.

He got out of the rental car and forced himself to walk slowly up the path and to the front porch. Fooling the NYPD and even Jade and Booker had been easy. No reason to blow it now with an old man who'd go down with a single punch, if it came to that.

The old man stood slowly and shuffled to the edge of the porch to meet him. "You looking for somebody?"

"As a matter of fact, I am." Javier extended a hand and introduced himself as they shook.

"I'm R.J., Jade's dad," the man said. "And you must be the friend of Quaid Vaquero who almost got murdered by the rotten scum who killed your friend."

"Your daughter and her friend Booker saved me. I owe them, big-time. I called Booker last night and told him I was in Dallas visiting friends. He told me to stop by anytime, so here I am."

"They didn't mention that to me and neither one of them is around right now. You can come in and wait, if you like. Might be a while. Or you can try to catch Jade at the horse barn. She and Hadley were going for a ride up to Shadow Junction. If you hurry you might catch them while they're still saddling up."

"Hope so. I'd love to join them for a ride. Where would I find the horse barn?"

"Follow that path behind the house. There're two barns. Not sure which horses they're taking, but you'll catch a glimpse of both barns as soon as you're out of sight of the house."

"Thanks.

"Guess you heard about the necklace…"

"What about it?"

"Oh, nothing. I have a tendency to talk too much."

And Javier was in no mood for listening.

He walked away but broke into a run the second he was out of the old man's view. Didn't want to do anything that might cause R.J. to have second thoughts about his showing up unannounced.

Not that the old guy could stop him, but he could call for one of his wranglers to run interference before Javier reached Jade.

With luck, this could be even easier than murdering Quaid had been.

But this time there could be no mistake. Javier was already pushing the time limits. He needed to leave the country before someone figured out that he was the one who'd killed Quaid. If that happened, he'd have to go without the necklace and the money that rightfully belonged to him and Zoe.

Jade had the necklace. She'd outsmarted them all. But she would never live to enjoy the wealth it would bring.

One chance. Now or never. It had taken much of the millions Javier had embezzled from Quaid over the years to fund his perfect escape. A chartered copter ride from the Dry Gulch to the private jet in Dallas and then on to Bora Bora.

All his years of kissing up to Quaid would finally come through for him.

Once Jade was dead and the necklace was in his hands.

"I'VE NEVER SEEN such serious faces. Are the cows causing trouble again?"

Booker looked up as Travis joined them in the ranch office.

"We are serious," Adam said. "Booker has not been fishing since he got here. We're thinking we need a man's day on the water if we can drag him away from Jade long enough to catch some trout."

"Sounds good. Today's my day off, the first one in two weeks—unless I get called in again."

"I can take a few hours off," Adam said. "I'll just have to look over the wranglers' schedule and make sure everything's covered."

"Count me in," Cannon said. "Booker?"

"I can't very well miss a trip planned in my honor."

"So, it's a go," Adam said. "I'll call Leif. Unless he's in court, he might be able to rearrange his schedule and join us."

"I have a couple of chores to take care of first," Cannon said, "so I'd best quit shooting the bull and get busy. Are you ready to go back to the house, Booker?"

"No, but I'll be along soon. I need to talk to Travis a few minutes since he's here."

"No problem," Travis said. "I'll run you back to the big house to pick up the extra fishing gear after we talk."

"What's on your mind?" Travis asked once Cannon and Adam had left the room.

"Javier Aranda."

"What about him?"

"He called last night. He's on his way to Dallas."

"Why's he coming here?"

"For starters, he says he wants to thank Jade and he has a gift for her, a piece of jewelry his sister made. But there's something about that guy that worries me and I think I've finally put my finger on it."

"Like what?"

"When Jade and I answered his frantic call for help and found Zoe tied to a chair, Javier's emotions seemed all wrong."

"Can you be a little clearer?"

"Zoe was clearly bordering on hysteria, but Javier showed very little emotion."

"I've seen that before," Travis said. "Some guys appear cool under pressure, but they've really just zoned out because their mind can't handle it."

"Maybe, but I'm telling you, he didn't seem all that concerned about Zoe. Looking back, it was almost like he was part of the setup."

"Now you're starting to worry me," Travis said.

"Figure into that the fact that when Reggie pulled the trigger, he switched his aim and shot at Jade, not Zoe."

"She was the one he thought had the necklace," Travis reminded him.

"Yes, but my first thought on arriving at that apartment building was that we were walking into a trap. We were, of course, but now I'm not sure the trap was all Reggie's doing. He and Javier could have been working together."

"You said originally that you thought Quaid's murder had to be set up by someone on the inside who knew the necklace was in his room."

"Right," Booker said. "And Jade originally said there was a third man."

"Which could have been Javier. I think you should call Detective Fielding and tell him what you just told me."

"I agree." But first he'd call Jade. Suddenly he ached to hear her voice.

R.J. answered the phone and relayed the bone-chilling message. Jade was with Javier, possibly at Shadow Junction.

"I'm taking the ATV," Booker said, already rushing for the door.

He was already in the driver's seat, his foot on the throttle, when Travis jumped on behind him. A second later, they were bouncing and bumping along the rough terrain at breakneck speed.

Some lousy bodyguard he'd turned out to be.

"I'M GOING TO take a short hike along the water's edge while you two talk," Hadley said.

Javier nodded and swatted at a web of gnats. "I appreciate that."

"You don't have to go," Jade assured her.

"I won't be gone long."

Jade wished she could tell Javier about the necklace being found, but she didn't trust him not to release news like that to the media.

"You've recovered from the trauma quite well," Javier said once Hadley had disappeared beyond a curve in the shallow river.

"I'm going on with my life," Jade said. "You should, too, and you should help Zoe do the same. Quaid's death hit her very hard, but she must learn to focus on the wonderful memories they shared."

"She'll be lost without him," Javier said. "That's what happens when the slave worships the master."

Slave. Master. "I'm not sure what you're saying."

"Zoe was the docile, obedient servant girl dutifully bowing, scraping and silently pining away for the love of the man who took all and gave only scraps in return."

"You can't mean that, Javier. Quaid was constantly remarking on how skilled Zoe was in following his designs. He said she helped with all the most delicate work. He truly appreciated her skill and dedication."

"Of course he did. It was her genius that made him. The designs were Zoe's," Javier said.

"You don't believe that."

"Oh, but I do. Quaid used my sister. Worse, he knew

she loved him and he rubbed her nose in it, flaunting the beautiful women he slept with the same as he was flaunting you."

"That can't be true. Why are you saying these things? Quaid was your friend."

"He had been my friend once. But forget Quaid. I have a gift for you."

"From Zoe?"

"No. Zoe furnished you with the necklace. This one is from me."

He reached into his pocket, pulled out a pistol and pointed it at her head. "I'm sorry it has to be this way, but the necklace rightly belonged to Zoe. You should never have taken it."

Jade backed up slowly as icy fear seeped into her veins. "The necklace was found yesterday, Javier. It was hidden inside the support posts for the mirror in Quaid's hotel suite. The NYPD have it now. They'll be holding a press conference anytime now to release that information."

"No more lies, Jade. Time's up."

He stepped toward her. She eased one step backward.

"Call Detective Fielding if you don't believe me. He'll tell you. The necklace is safe. It will go back to Quaid's estate. I'm sure Zoe will get her share. You'd be killing me for nothing."

"You never give up, do you? It's an admirable quality, but it won't save you this time."

She wondered if she dared run. But then he'd come after her and might kill Hadley in the process. Hadley with her beautiful daughters. She couldn't let that happen. She needed a weapon—or a miracle.

She needed Booker.

"Sorry, Jade, but this is it."

Adrenaline hit like lightning. Jade dived toward Javier,

tackling him around his ankles. Gunfire exploded. She could hear Hadley's scream in the distance.

"Stay back," Jade called. "Please stay back.

"I don't have the necklace," Jade repeated, though it was clear Javier did not believe her.

"Then you will die."

She'd die in the shadows on an isolated spot on the Dry Gulch without ever telling Booker that she loved him. She'd found herself only to lose her life. She should have never come back to the ranch.

THE ATV BUMPED and bounced along the uneven ground, jarring every bone in Booker's body as he raced along the uneven line of trees that edged the river.

Travis pointed the way. Dread tore at Booker's control. He was trained to handle emergencies, practiced in facing danger without fear.

He'd faced death without blinking an eye, yet he'd never felt the icy panic that clawed at his insides now.

He'd failed Jade, the one woman he loved more than he'd ever dreamed he could love a woman. He could no longer imagine life without her.

The whir of a helicopter sounded over the hammering of his heart and the growling roar of the ATV's motor. It was heading in the same direction they were going, but much faster. He watched it, saw it slow and then hover a couple of hundred yards in front of them.

It had to be here for Javier's escape after he'd killed Jade. A pain as sharp as a jagged-edged sword pushed through the Booker's heart. Please don't let him be too late.

The crack of gunfire cut through the deafening roar of the chopper and the grinding of the ATV's engine.

Terror ripped through Booker as if he were the one the bullet had found.

He spotted Hadley then, her mass of fiery red curls flowing behind her, her boots kicking up mud as she raced toward the copter. He and Travis yelled in unison for her to hang back and take cover. He didn't slow down to see if she'd heeded or even heard their warning.

Booker finally spotted Javier standing in front of the witch's cabin. His heart shattered when he spotted Jade on the ground at his feet.

Booker threw on the brakes and jumped from the ATV as the helicopter lowered.

Javier didn't turn around or show any sign he knew Booker and Travis were there. The deafening beating of the rotor blades had obviously drowned out their approach. Javier hadn't seen them, but apparently the copter pilot had.

The copter began to pull away. Javier waved his arms frantically. The copter paid no heed. As it withdrew, Javier turned. A look of panic crossed his face as he leaned over, grabbed Jade's arm and yanked her up so that she was standing in front of him.

Booker gasped for air. Jade was alive. The gunshot must have been to summon the waiting helicopter. But now the copter was gone and Javier's pistol was pointed at her head.

"Make a move toward me and she's history," Javier said.

"If you plan on killing Jade, I hope you have a very good reason for doing it," Travis said, finally getting into the act. "It's two against one, both of us sharpshooters. There's no way you're going to walk away from this alive."

"Put your gun down," Booker urged. "You haven't

killed anyone yet, Javier. Keep it that way, and you'll not only live but will get to see Spain and your sister again."

"He thinks I have the necklace," Jade said. "I told him the NYPD has it, but he doesn't believe me."

"Killing Jade won't help you get the necklace. All it will do is get you killed or imprisoned for life. Drop it without hurting Jade and we'll drive off and leave you to call for the copter again."

"Unless you ever show your face back in my town again," Travis added.

Javier looked as if he was considering the offer, but then his expression changed and Booker knew he was going to fire. Without taking a breath, Booker aimed and shot.

The gunshots from their two pistols were almost simultaneous, but miraculously Booker's made contact first, hitting Javier in the gun hand just in time to spoil his aim.

Javier let out a howl as the pistol fell from his mangled fingers.

Booker rushed to Jade and pulled her into his arms. "Are you okay?"

"I'm fine, thanks to my bodyguard."

"You almost gave me a heart attack, Jade Dalton. I've faced five terrorists at once and wasn't this scared."

"Really? I wasn't scared at all after you arrived." She reached up and fingered the SEAL Trident around his neck.

"Then you had a lot more faith than I did," Booker whispered.

"That's what's great about loving a Navy SEAL. I do love you, Booker. I love you very, very much."

"And I love you."

More than life itself. And whatever it took, he never wanted to come this close to losing her again.

Two weeks later, Jade and Booker stood on the front porch of the big house with Cannon and R.J., saying their goodbyes as the last of the family left to go back to their homes after a going-away party for Booker.

"How about a moonlit walk to top off the evening?" Booker said to Jade when R.J. went back inside.

"On one condition."

"Name it and I'll see if I can comply."

"No more talk of Javier or Quaid or anything to do with the danger that's past. Not that I'm in any way tired of your being hailed as a hero, but I just don't want to deal with that tonight."

"Fine by me. As any Navy SEAL will tell you, heroes are just targets that were missed."

His SEAL team was the other thing she should have made conversational taboo. He'd be leaving this weekend, in just three more days. She'd known that day would come from the very beginning, but now that it was almost time, she didn't see how she'd face it.

So maybe she wouldn't. She was a Dalton. She didn't have to accept the seemingly inevitable without putting up a fight. The black negligee and gold stilettos might have to come out of the closet tonight.

Number three had always said if you couldn't beat them, join them. She doubted that when he said it, he'd had the US Special Forces in mind.

She linked her arm with Booker's. "No wonder you love being a Navy SEAL. You thrive on danger."

"I like to think of it as being a little more meaningful than that, more like helping to keep our country safe.

But I admit I can't see myself pushing a pencil around all day."

"Not you, Booker. Not ever."

"I'd make a lousy husband. My headquarters is Coronado, California, but my team's field of operations is the Middle East. Bottom line, I'm almost never in any place I could call home. A wife of mine would have to very independent."

"You mean like me?"

"Yeah, but things will be better when I retire after a few more tours of duty. Might even be fun to live somewhere like the Dry Gulch Ranch, you know, if my wife wanted to live there."

Jade stopped walking. She might not need that negligee tonight after all. "Is this a proposal, Booker Knox?"

"An attempt at one."

"It's about time."

"Then I don't want to screw it up too bad." He fell to one knee. "Will you marry me, Jade? I love the way you kiss, the way you make love, the way you look when you wake up with your tousled hair haloing across the pillow. I love the way you laugh, the way you strut in those nosebleed heels and in the cowboy boots. I just plain love everything about you.

"If you say no, I'm probably going to stalk you until you change your mind or for the rest of your life, whichever comes first."

"No use to beg, cowboy. You had me from the second kiss."

"You never mentioned that to me."

"I didn't want to frighten you off before you realized how much you loved me."

"Guess you knew I'd come around since I was so crazy about you I couldn't keep my hands off you?"

"There was that, but you never really had a chance. Apparently when a Dalton woman goes after her man, failure is never an option."

THE WEDDING OF Jade Dalton and Booker Knox was solemnized one night before they left for California with the promise to return to the Dry Gulch Ranch every chance they got.

R.J. Dalton gave his only daughter, Jade, away at an altar beneath the stars on the side lawn of the Dry Gulch Ranch. Even with such short notice the entire Dalton family, the bride's mother and dozens of the Daltons' neighbors were in attendance.

Everyone said they had never seen a happier couple.

And it had all started with two strangers and a kiss.

* * * * *

COMING NEXT MONTH FROM

HARLEQUIN

INTRIGUE

Available May 19, 2015

#1569 TO HONOR AND TO PROTECT
The Specialists: Heroes Next Door
by Debra Webb & Regan Black
Addison Collins will do anything to protect her son. But can she protect her heart from former Army special forces operative Andrew Bryant, the man who left her at the altar—and the only one she can trust to safeguard their son?

#1570 NAVY SEAL NEWLYWED
Covert Cowboys, Inc. • by Elle James
Posing as newlyweds, Navy SEAL "Rip" Cord Schafer and Covert Cowboy operative Tracie Kosart work together to catch the traitors supplying guns to terrorists. But when Tracie's cover is blown, can Rip save his "wife"?

#1571 CORNERED
Corcoran Team: Bulletproof Bachelors
by HelenKay Dimon
Former Navy pilot Cameron Roth has no plans to settle down. When drug runners set their sights on Julia White, it is up to Cam to get them both out alive...

#1572 THE GUARDIAN
The Ranger Brigade • by Cindi Myers
Veteran Abby Stewart has no memory of Rangers lieutenant Michael Dance, who saved her life in Afghanistan. But when she stumbles into his investigation, can he save her from the smugglers stalking them?

#1573 UNTRACEABLE
Omega Sector • by Janie Crouch
After a brutal attack leaves her traumatized, a powerful crime boss forces Omega Sector agent Juliet Branson undercover again. Now, Evan Karcz must neutralize the terrorist threat and use his cover as Juliet's husband to rehabilitate her.

#1574 SECURITY BREACH
Bayou Bonne Chance • by Mallory Kane
Undercover Homeland Security agent Tristan DuChaud faked his death to protect his pregnant wife, Sandy, from terrorists. But when her life is threatened, Tristan is forced to tell her the truth—or risk both their deaths becoming reality...

HICNM0515

REQUEST YOUR FREE BOOKS!
2 FREE NOVELS PLUS 2 FREE GIFTS!

HARLEQUIN®

INTRIGUE

BREATHTAKING ROMANTIC SUSPENSE

YES! Please send me 2 FREE Harlequin® Intrigue novels and my 2 FREE gifts (gifts are worth about $10). After receiving them, if I don't wish to receive any more books, I can return the shipping statement marked "cancel." If I don't cancel, I will receive 6 brand-new novels every month and be billed just $4.74 per book in the U.S. or $5.49 per book in Canada. That's a savings of at least 12% off the cover price! It's quite a bargain! Shipping and handling is just 50¢ per book in the U.S. and 75¢ per book in Canada.* I understand that accepting the 2 free books and gifts places me under no obligation to buy anything. I can always return a shipment and cancel at any time. Even if I never buy another book, the two free books and gifts are mine to keep forever.

182/382 HDN GH3D

Name _____ (PLEASE PRINT) _____

Address _____ Apt. #

City _____ State/Prov. _____ Zip/Postal Code

Signature (if under 18, a parent or guardian must sign)

Mail to the **Reader Service:**
IN U.S.A.: P.O. Box 1867, Buffalo, NY 14240-1867
IN CANADA: P.O. Box 609, Fort Erie, Ontario L2A 5X3

Are you a subscriber to Harlequin® Intrigue books and want to receive the larger-print edition?
Call 1-800-873-8635 or visit www.ReaderService.com.

* Terms and prices subject to change without notice. Prices do not include applicable taxes. Sales tax applicable in N.Y. Canadian residents will be charged applicable taxes. Offer not valid in Quebec. This offer is limited to one order per household. Not valid for current subscribers to Harlequin Intrigue books. All orders subject to credit approval. Credit or debit balances in a customer's account(s) may be offset by any other outstanding balance owed by or to the customer. Please allow 4 to 6 weeks for delivery. Offer available while quantities last.

Your Privacy—The Reader Service is committed to protecting your privacy. Our Privacy Policy is available online at www.ReaderService.com or upon request from the Reader Service.

We make a portion of our mailing list available to reputable third parties that offer products we believe may interest you. If you prefer that we not exchange your name with third parties, or if you wish to clarify or modify your communication preferences, please visit us at www.ReaderService.com/consumerchoice or write to us at Reader Service Preference Service, P.O. Box 9062, Buffalo, NY 14240-9062. Include your complete name and address.

HI15

SPECIAL EXCERPT FROM

HARLEQUIN

INTRIGUE

Navy SEAL "Rip" Cord Schafer's mission is not a one-man operation, but never in his wildest dreams did he imagine teaming up with a woman: Covert Cowboy operative Tracie Kosart.

Read on for a sneak peek of
NAVY SEAL NEWLYWED,
the newest installment from Elle James's
COVERT COWBOYS, INC.

"How do I know you really work for Hank?"

"You don't. But has anyone else shown up and told you he's your contact?" She raised her eyebrows, the saucy expression doing funny things to his insides. "So, do you trust me, or not?"

His lips curled upward on the ends. "I'll go with not."

"Oh, come on, sweetheart." She batted her pretty green eyes and gave him a sexy smile. "What's not to trust?"

His gaze scraped over her form. "I expected a cowboy, not a…"

"Cow*girl*?" Her smile sank and she slipped into the driver's seat. Her lips firmed into a straight line. "Are you coming or not? If you're dead set on a cowboy, I'll contact Hank and tell him to send a male replacement. But then he'd have to come up with another plan."

"I'm interested in how you and Hank plan to help. Frankly, I'd rather my SEAL team had my six."

"Yeah, but you're deceased. Using your SEAL team

would only alert your assassin that you aren't as dead as the navy claims you are. How long do you think you'll last once that bit of news leaks out?"

His lips pressed together. "I'd survive."

"By going undercover? Then you still won't have the backing of your team, and we're back to the original plan." She grinned. "Me."

Rip sighed. "Fine. I want to head back to Honduras and trace the weapons back to where they're coming from. What's Hank's plan?"

"For me to work with you." She pulled a large envelope from between her seat and the console and handed it across to him. "Everything we need is in that packet."

Rip riffled through the contents of the packet, glancing at a passport with his picture on it as well as a name he'd never seen. "Chuck Gideon?"

"Better get used to it."

"Speaking of names…we've already kissed and you haven't told me who you are." Rip glanced her way briefly. "Is it a secret? Do you have a shady past or are you related to someone important?"

"For this mission, I'm related to someone important." She twisted her lips and sent a crooked grin his way. "You. For the purpose of this operation, you can call me Phyllis. Phyllis Gideon. I'll be your wife."

Don't miss
NAVY SEAL NEWLYWED
available June 2015 wherever
Harlequin Intrigue® books and ebooks are sold.

www.Harlequin.com

Love the Harlequin book you just read?

Your opinion matters.

Review this book on your favorite
book site, review site, blog or your own
social media properties and share
your opinion with other readers!

Be sure to connect with us at:
Harlequin.com/Newsletters
Facebook.com/HarlequinBooks
Twitter.com/HarlequinBooks

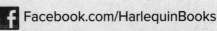
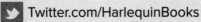

THE WORLD IS BETTER WITH

Romance

Harlequin has everything from contemporary, passionate and heartwarming to suspenseful and inspirational stories.

Whatever your mood,
we have a romance just for you!

Connect with us to find your next great read, special offers and more.

f /HarlequinBooks

🐦 @HarlequinBooks

www.HarlequinBlog.com

www.Harlequin.com/Newsletters

♦ HARLEQUIN®

A *Romance* FOR EVERY MOOD™

www.Harlequin.com

HARLEQUIN®

A *Romance* FOR EVERY MOOD™

**Stay up-to-date on all your
romance-reading news with the
Harlequin Shopping Guide,
featuring bestselling authors, exciting new
miniseries, books to watch and more!**

The newest issue will be delivered right to you
with our compliments! There are 4 each year.

Signing up is easy.

EMAIL

ShoppingGuide@Harlequin.ca

WRITE TO US

HARLEQUIN BOOKS
Attention: Customer Service Department
P.O. Box 9057, Buffalo, NY 14269-9057

OR PHONE

1-800-873-8635 in the United States
1-888-343-9777 in Canada

Please allow 4-6 weeks for delivery of the first issue by mail.